Z

Slough   01753 535166   Langley   01753 542153
ippenham   01628 661745   Britwell   01753 522869

ease return/renew this item by the last date shown.
ns may also be renewed by phone and internet.

www.slough.gov.uk
ough
Council

LIB/3296/08-12-06

D1331720

MR ZERO

PATRICIA WENTWORTH

ISIS
LARGE PRINT
Oxford

Copyright © J. B. Lippincott Company, 1938

First published in Great Britain 1938
by
Hodder & Stoughton

Published in Large Print 2011 by ISIS Publishing Ltd.,
7 Centremead, Osney Mead, Oxford OX2 0ES
by arrangement with
Andrew Nurnberg Associates

British Library Cataloguing in Publication Data
Wentworth, Patricia.
    Mr Zero.
    1. Extortion - - Fiction.
    2. Women gamblers - - Fiction.
    3. Great Britain - - Officials and employees - -
    Fiction.
    4. Murder - - Investigation - - Fiction.
    5. Detective and mystery stories.
    6. Large type books.
    I. Title
    823.9'12–dc22

ISBN 978–0–7531–8908–5 (hb)
ISBN 978–0–7531–8909–2 (pb)

Printed and bound in Great Britain by
T. J. International Ltd., Padstow, Cornwall

CHAPTER
ONE

The telephone bell rang, and went on ringing. Miss Agatha Hardwicke kept her instrument in the front hall where everyone could hear every single word that was said. If the postman came while you were talking, or a caller, or an errand boy, he, she or it was also included in the audience. And if you happened to be in your bedroom five floors up, you had to run all the way down and arrive breathless.

Gay Hardwicke arrived breathless. "If it's anyone else about that blighted bazaar, I'll smash you!" she said, and jammed the receiver against one ear. With the other she heard the kitchen door open at the foot of the basement stair. That meant that Mrs Hollings was listening in. She always did when Gay telephoned, and Gay didn't really mind, because Holly was an old pet and so passionately interested in her affairs. She probably wouldn't listen for very long this time, because it was a female voice that said,

"Miss Hardwicke — can I speak to Miss Hardwicke?"

"Miss Hardwicke is out, I'm afraid."

Why Aunt Agatha couldn't be at home to take her own blighted calls about her own blighted bazaar instead of having them just when one was half way through washing one's hair —

But the telephone had suddenly become eager and explanatory.

"Gay — *darling* — is that you? Your voice sounded all woofly —"

"So would yours if you had to run down five flights of stairs every time Aunt Agatha's League of Help thought of a new pattern for a pincushion."

"My poor angel — how grim! It's Marcia Thrale speaking."

"Yes, I got that. Where are you?"

"Well, it's too marvellous — darling, I must see you — I'm at the Luxe."

"What on earth are you doing at the Luxe?"

"Well, it's simply *too* marvellous. You know my Uncle George?"

"Is that the one in Java, or the one who could never keep a job in South America?"

"No, that was Denis. He's Mummy's brother — on the other side. This is the one in Java, George Thrale, and he's got pots of money, and he's my godfather, and after sending me a christening mug three years running he stopped doing anything about it till a fortnight ago, and then he sent Mummy a cheque for three hundred pounds and said, 'Get her all the proper clothes and let her come out with my friends the Middletons who are sailing on the fifth of Feb.'"

"But, Marcia, that's tomorrow!"

"I know, darling. And that's positively all there was in the letter, except 'Dear Mary' at the beginning and

'Cable reply. Love. George' at the end. Gay, I *must* speak to you. What are you doing?"

"Well, I was trying to wash my hair. It's dripping all over the hall table at this minute."

"Darling, how *grim!* Jane told me you were with your Aunt Agatha — but why? The last I heard, you were going to Madeira."

"It wouldn't run to it," said Gay mournfully. "Daddy and Mummy had to go because someone's started a lawsuit about Mummy's property out there. If it doesn't come out all right, there'll be frightfully little money, so when Aunt Agatha offered to have me they said 'Thank you very much, kind sister' and dumped me."

"Darling, how *utterly* grim!"

Gay sparkled at her end of the line. Even with her black curls wet and dripping and an old school dressing-gown pulled hastily round her, she didn't look at all like the sort of girl who would sit down and play Cinderella whilst her parents basked in the sun. Aunt Agatha was a bore, and bazaars were a bore, but there were compensations. She said,

"Oh — well —"

Marcia pounced.

"What does that mean?"

Gay made a little impudent face. Her nose wrinkled and her dark eyes danced.

"*Very* kind-hearted people sometimes take me out," she said.

Marcia giggled.

3

"Don't I know it! You're that sort, you little wretch."
Then, with a sudden change of tone, "Get your hair dry
and come round. I've got to see you."

Gay drew back an inch or two. Something said,
"*Don't go.*" The words were so loud and distinct in her
mind that she very nearly dropped the receiver. She
stood there frowning at it, her gay, bright colour gone
as if a puff of wind had blown it out — a wind of fear
— a cold, cold wind of dread.

"Gay — where are you — are you there?"

Gay said, "Yes." The wind went past her and was
gone. The fear was gone. Her colour came back.

"Gay — what's the matter? You sounded — funny."

Gay laughed her own gay laugh.

"I went all cold. There's a beast of a draught under
Aunt Agatha's front door. Why do you want me to
come round?"

Marcia giggled.

"Darling, what a thing to ask! I want to see you of
course."

Gay frowned again.

"Why do you want me?" Marcia *didn't*, unless there
was something you could do for her.

Marcia stopped giggling. She said imploringly.

"Oh, Gay, do come! It's about Sylvia — she's in an
awful jam."

CHAPTER
TWO

"Sylvia's such an idiot," said Marcia Thrale with a giggle.

"She always was," said Gay. She didn't giggle, she frowned. She was remembering all the different times Sylvia had been an idiot, and had got in a jam, and had had to be hauled out again. And it wasn't Marcia who had done the hauling, though she was her sister, it was nearly always Gay Hardwicke. And a jam at school was one thing, but a jam after you are married and ought to be living happy ever after was quite another. Her frown deepened, and she said impatiently, "What on earth has she been doing now?"

They were in Marcia Thrale's bedroom at the Luxe. It was a riotous orgy of pink. Everything that could be pink had been painted, upholstered, or draped in that colour. Mercifully, a good deal of it was obscured by the boxes, the dresses, the hats, coats, shoes, stockings, and gloves which Marcia was taking to Java. Gay had firmly made a place for herself on the edge of the rose-coloured bed, Marcia, in a pink satin dressing-gown, having already annexed the only armchair. Marcia was like that. It ran in the family, because Sylvia was like it too — only more so. But then Sylvia was lovely, and everyone had always spoiled her. Marcia wasn't bad-looking when you saw her away from Sylvia, but nobody would ever look at her if they could look at Sylvia instead, so Marcia hadn't really got the same excuse.

Gay tossed back her damp black curls and said,

"What on earth is it this time?"

Marcia spoke comfortably from the chair.

"Well, you know what Sylvia is. She never writes — at least only postcards to Mummy, because if she didn't do that, she'd have Mummy ringing up every other day to know if she was dead."

"Yes?" said Gay. You couldn't hurry Marcia, but you could try.

"I don't think I've had a single letter from her since she was married, and that's just on a year ago. And I've only *seen* her at home, when she rushed down for about half an hour, and of course Mummy was there the whole time. But I lunched with her yesterday — to say goodbye, you know — and she told me she was in this awful jam. She really did look pretty ghastly. I mean she'd got on the wrong stockings for her dress, and her lipstick all crooked, so I think things are pretty grim."

"What is it?" said Gay, in a resigned tone.

Marcia waved a newly manicured hand.

"Darling, she never told me. We only had about ten minutes after lunch, and the moment she began I said quite firmly, 'Well, my dear, it's no good your asking *me* to do anything, because I'm absolutely up to my eyes and sailing day after tomorrow at some ghastly

6

hour like cock-crow.' And she was just beginning to go all orphan-of-the-storm, when Francis came in, and she dried right up and got rid of me as soon as she possibly could — I can't think why. I wouldn't have married Francis if he'd been fifty times as rich, but we've always got on all right."

Gay laughed.

"Considering Sylvia had only known him for six weeks before they got married and you were away for quite half that time —"

Marcia giggled.

"It didn't give me a chance, did it? But I really wouldn't have married him even if Sylvia hadn't got off with him first."

"Well, I've only seen him twice. He seemed all right. Isn't he being nice to Sylvia?"

"Oh, I don't think it's that," said Marcia. She got up, stretched herself, and gathered the pink dressing-gown round her. "Darling, I've got one last fitting. Such a bore! It's the pink crepe. *Mercifully*, I tried it on when it came at lunch-time, and the hem is *crooked*. I told Madame Frederica exactly what I thought about it on the telephone, and she fairly crawled, so she's sending a girl to do it here, and Mrs Middleton says I can use her room, because it's got a much better glass than this." She got as far as the door, yawned, and said over her shoulder, "So you can see Sylvia here."

Gay leapt from the rose-coloured eiderdown, caught Marcia by a pink satin shoulder, and shook it vigorously.

"Sylvia? My good girl, what are you talking about?"

7

Marcia's rather light blue eyes opened widely.

"Darling, didn't I tell you? She's coming here on purpose to see you. That's why I wanted you to come."

"Sylvia's coming here to see me?"

"Yes, darling. Didn't I tell you?"

Gay stamped an angry foot.

"You know very well you didn't! It's a plant! You're wriggling out and landing me with Sylvia exactly like you always did at school!"

Marcia giggled faintly.

"Darling, somebody's got to help her, and I'm going to Java."

Gay let go of the pink shoulder and stood back.

"When is she coming?"

Marcia looked at a new wrist-watch.

"Well, she's due now, but she's always late."

"Why is she coming here? If she wants to see me, why can't she come and see me? Why drag me here?"

"Really, darling — *drag!* And we had to get you here because of Francis! You see, even Francis couldn't think there was anything odd about Sylvia coming to say goodbye to me before I go to Java. At least, I think he might if he knew her as well as we do, but I don't suppose he does — not about things like that. Now look here, she really does rely on you to help her, because when I was coming away yesterday she simply gripped my hand and said, 'Where's Gay? I *must* see her. Do let me know where she is.' And she couldn't say any more than that, because Francis was there, but she pinched my hand till I very nearly screamed, so I thought I'd better find you and let her know. And the

8

minute she heard you were coming, she said she'd dash round in a taxi — and I expect that's she."

The telephone bell rang from the pink pedestal beside the bed. Marcia took up the receiver, listened for a moment, and spoke into it.

"Lady Colesborough? . . . Oh, yes, I'm expecting her. Please send her up." She turned to see Gay reaching for her hat.

"You can see Sylvia yourself, Marcia."

Marcia's colour rose.

"Darling, you can't go — you *can't!* She's come here on purpose to see you. You *can't!*"

"Watch me!" said Gay. She snapped out the words, shut down her lips in a determined scarlet line, and pulled up the collar of her dark grey coat.

"Oh, Gay!"

Something in Gay said, "Run for it!" and she ran. But before she had taken a dozen steps along the corridor she was pulled up short. Sylvia Colesborough was coming towards her — Sylvia pale and lovely, with her golden hair under a little grey cap, and a pale grey squirrel coat falling open over a dress of pale grey wool. She said, "Oh, Gay!" in her lovely helpless voice, and Gay knew that it was too late to run away. Whatever Sylvia Colesborough's trouble was, it was going to be Gay Hardwicke's trouble from now onwards.

She went back into Marcia's room with Sylvia, and found it empty. A little bright flame of rage flickered up in Gay. It burned in her cheeks and set a dancing spark in her eyes. She looked at Sylvia in the pink brocade chair and said,

"What on earth have you been up to?"

Sylvia Colesborough was taking off her grey suede gloves, frowning a little because the third left-hand finger had caught itself up on the big diamond in her engagement ring. It was a very big diamond, a single stone surrounded by fine brilliants. The gloves were very expensive gloves. Sylvia laid them in her lap and folded her hands upon them. She was wearing a pale rose lipstick and nail-polish, and green eye-shadow, but she had the sense to leave her eyelashes alone. Nature had painted them a full six tones deeper than her flax-gold hair, and, lavishly generous, had tipped the curling ends with gold. It was these lashes and the almost midnight blue of the eyes they screened which gave to Sylvia's beauty a certain exquisite strangeness.

She lifted those lovely eyes and said,

"Oh, Gay!"

Gay tapped with her foot upon the rose-coloured carpet.

"That gets us a lot farther, doesn't it!" she said.

"But, Gay darling, Marcia said —"

"Marcia would! She always did fob you off on to me when she got half a chance!"

A sweet, fleeting smile touched Sylvia's lips.

"Darling, you were so clever. You always got me out of things. I've always said you're the cleverest person I know. You will help me, won't you?"

Gay leaned against the ornamental rail at the bottom of the bed, a rail of rose-coloured enamel with bright gilt knobs.

"Now look here, Sylvia, why should I help you? We were at school together, I was your bridesmaid, and you're some sort of fifteenth cousin. You've never written me a line since you got married, you've never been near me since I came to London, and I've never been inside your house —"

"Oh, but I didn't know —"

"Oh, yes, you did, because I wrote and told you — I told you Mummy and Daddy were going to Madeira and marooning me with Aunt Agatha. And did you rally round? Not a rally! Did you take the trouble to lift the receiver from that mother-of-pearl telephone thing you had for one of your wedding presents and coo into it, 'Darling, do come round and see me'? You know you didn't. Sylvia, if you look at me like that, I'll throw something at you — I really will!"

Sylvia's lovely eyes had widened piteously. A clear, round tear brimmed gently over and rolled quite slowly and with immense effect down a faintly tinted cheek. Gay's little angry flame burned higher. If Sylvia would only get cross — but Sylvia never got cross. You might call her the most awful names, and she didn't resent them, or hate you. She just cried, and made you feel what a brute you were. She was making Gay feel like that now. A tear rolled down the other cheek too. She didn't wipe either of them away, she just let them fall on to the pale grey gloves, and said in a lost-child sort of voice.

"I know — I've been horrid. There isn't any reason why you should help me, only — I'm so frightened, and I don't know what to do — I don't indeed." The tears were falling faster now. They welled up, ran over, and fell. They kept on falling. They put out Gay's little angry flame. She would have to take a hand. She had known that all the time of course. You can't just let an idiotic creature down because it doesn't know enough to come in out of the rain. She tossed back her hair and said,

"Oh, I'll help you. You always knew I would. Stop crying, Silly Billy baby, and tell me what it's all about. Whatever have you been and gone and done?"

CHAPTER
THREE

Sylvia drew a long sighing breath, dabbed her eyes with a mauve handkerchief, and opened a grey suede bag with a diamond initial on it.

Gay cocked her eye at it.

"Wedding present?" she enquired.

"No — Francis — for Christmas. Rather nice, isn't it?" From an inner pocket she produced a scrap of newspaper. "There — you'd better read it."

The piece of paper was about five inches long and two inches wide. It looked as if it had been torn off the edge of the *Times*. On the blank margin there was scrawled in pencil:

"Same place. Same time. Same money."

The words stood one below the other like the rungs of a ladder, the letters coarsely printed with a blunt blue pencil. Gay frowned at them.

"What does it mean?"

"I didn't go," said Sylvia in a tired voice. "Then I got this one."

She fished out another piece of newspaper. A tear splashed down on it and smudged the blue pencil, but it was legible enough. In the same coarse scrawl Gay read:

"Tomorrow without fail, or your husband will know."

Her lips tightened. What an absolute first-class prize idiot Sylvia was.

"Look here, Sylly, it's no good beating about the bush. What have you been doing that Francis mustn't know? Is it another man?"

"Oh, *no!*" said Sylvia. "Oh, no — really not, darling. I — I *wouldn't!*"

Gay was a good deal relieved, because if there wasn't another man, the obvious thing to do was to tell Francis Colesborough and get him to wring this blackmailing creature's neck. She said so with a good deal of vigour. A vivid little creature in spite of the dark grey coat and black beret. Eyes, colour and lips were all alive as she pointed out the folly of practising concealments from your husband.

"You go straight home and tell him and you won't have any more trouble."

Sylvia paled visibly, clasped and unclasped her hands, and appeared completely panic-stricken.

"Oh, Gay — I couldn't!"

"Why couldn't you?"

"Oh, Gay, I couldn't — I really *couldn't!*"

Gay leaned back against the bed. What was it all about? She said,

"Sylvia, what's Francis like?"

Because, after all, that was what really mattered. You *could* tell things to some people, and you couldn't tell them to others. Everything really depended on what Francis was like.

Sylvia responded with a slightly puzzled air.

"Well, he's tall — and fair — and —"

"Yes — I saw him at the wedding, and that time at Cole Lester. But I don't want to know what size collar he takes, or what his handicap is at golf — I want to know what he's like in himself."

"Well, he's much older than I am. Let me see — you and Marcia are the same age — and Marcia is twenty — and I'm two years older — so I'm twenty-two — and Francis was twenty years older than me when we married — and that was a year ago —"

Gay looked at her almost with awe.

"In fact, he's forty-two. Sylly, can't you really remember how old you are without counting up from Marcia and me?"

"You're so good at figures," said Sylvia in a helpless tone.

The conversation seemed to have slid right away from Francis. That was what happened when you tried to talk to Sylvia — you slipped, and slid, and didn't get anywhere at all. Gay made a determined attempt to get back to Francis.

"We weren't really talking about how old anyone was. I don't care whether Francis is fourteen, or forty, or four hundred. I want to know what he's like to live with. Is he fond of you — is he nice to you — are you fond of him?"

Sylvia smiled a little consciously.

"Oh, well, he's in love with me."

"People aren't always nice to you when they're in love with you." Gay was remembering Julian Carr who had made such a frightful scene when she said she wouldn't marry him. "And they're not always fond of you either." And she didn't know how she knew that, but she did know it.

"It's the same thing," said Sylvia in a puzzled voice.

"You're very lucky if it is," said Gay with a wisdom beyond her years. "But if it really is the same thing with Francis, then you haven't got to bother at all, because you can just go straight home and tell him, and he can deal with the blue pencil — stamp on it, or push its face in. Anyhow you won't have to bother any more."

Sylvia looked lovely and mournful. She shook her head.

"It wouldn't do at all, darling."

"Why wouldn't it?"

"Oh, it *wouldn't*. You don't know Francis."

Gay blew up.

"Is that my fault? I keep asking you what he's like, and you're about as much use as a jelly that hasn't jelled! *Why* wouldn't it do to tell Francis?"

Sylvia appeared to reflect. The unusual effort brought a tiny line to her white brow.

"He'd be angry," she said at last.

"That won't hurt you," said Gay. "You'd much better tell him."

Sylvia shook her head again.

"I can't."

"I'll do it for you if you like," said Gay handsomely. "I could do it most awfully well, because I could begin by telling him that you were the world's prize fool and couldn't help getting into some mess or other. And then I could tell him about this particular mess — and

16

of course he'd see that it was up to him to get you out of it."

Sylvia stood up, and stood trembling. It was as if she had begun to run away and then lost heart, or strength, or nerve — perhaps all three. She said with twitching lips,

"Don't tell him! Don't — don't — *don't!*"

Gay came over to her and put her back in her chair.

"Sit down," she said, "and don't be an ass. To begin with, I don't know anything to tell, and to go on with —"

Sylvia clutched at her wrist.

"You mustn't tell Francis! If I could tell him, I wouldn't have come to you. Promise me you won't ever tell."

"I won't promise," said Gay soberly, "but I won't tell." She removed her wrist and stood back again. "The question is, are you going to tell *me?* Because if you're not, I'll be getting along."

The faint, lovely colour returned to Sylvia's cheek. She drew a long breath and sat back.

"Oh, darling, don't go! I *want* to tell you."

"Then get on with it," said Gay.

Sylvia looked up, and down again.

"It's so difficult. You see, one of the reasons I can't tell Francis is that he said I was never, never, never to play cards for money. They play a lot, you know, in his set, and the points are dreadfully high, and he said I wasn't to ever, because — well, it was after he'd been my partner one night at contract and we lost eight hundred pounds, and he said he wasn't a millionaire,

17

and even if he was he couldn't bear the strain, and a lot of things like that."

Gay felt some sympathy for Francis Colesborough. She had played cards with Sylvia at school.

"Did you revoke?" she enquired with interest.

Sylvia gazed at her mournfully.

"I expect so — I generally do. I never can remember what it is exactly, but that is one of the things he said I'd done. So he said I wasn't to play again."

"And you did?"

"Not bridge — baccarat."

"And how much did you lose?" It went without saying that Sylvia had lost.

"About five hundred pounds," said Sylvia in a small, terrified voice. If she was now the wife of the rich Sir Francis Colesborough and mistress of Cole Lester, she had spent twenty-one years as penniless Sylvia Thrale with a widowed mother whose tiny pension had only just sufficed to feed and clothe herself and her two daughters. Relations had most unwillingly paid the school bills. Sylvia had therefore always heard a great deal about money — bills and the lack of money to pay them with; bills and the sordid necessity of paying them; bills and the horrid things that might happen to you if you didn't pay them. All this had been impressed upon her in the nursery.

"*What!* said Gay. And then, "But you'll *have* to tell Francis. He's the only person who can help you to pay five hundred pounds." Sylvia shook her head.

"Oh, no, he isn't — that's just it."

Long practice enabled Gay to snatch the meaning from this remark.

"You mean someone else gave you the money, and that's why you can't tell Francis?"

"Only half," said Sylvia, accepting this interpretation.

"This blue pencil creature?"

"I don't know."

Gay stamped her foot.

"You don't know who gave you the money?"

"No, darling."

A kind of furious calm possessed Gay.

"Sylvia, if you don't tell me the whole thing right away, I'm off. No, don't bleat — begin at the beginning and go right on to the end. You lost five hundred pounds at baccarat. Now begin there, and get a move on!"

The line came again on Sylvia's forehead.

"Someone rang me up —"

"When?"

"Last week-end — last Saturday — because we were going down to stay with the Wessex-Gardners. At least, I was going, and Francis was going to come if he could, and he did, only rather late for dinner — we were half way through the fish."

Gay broke in.

"Sylly, for goodness' sake —"

Sylvia stared in surprise.

"So I know it was Saturday. And the bell rang whilst I was dressing. I was all ready except for my fur coat, so I expect it was about five o'clock."

"Good girl! Go on — keep on going on! Someone rang you up —"

"Yes. They said —"

"Who said?"

"Well, it was a man — and he said would I like to earn two hundred pounds."

"*Earn* two hundred pounds?"

"That's what he said. And I said of course, so then he told me how."

A feeling of the blackest dismay came seeping into Gay's mind. It was like ink seeping into blotting-paper. What on earth had Sylvia done? She said,

"What did he tell you?"

"How to do it," said Sylvia. "It was quite easy really."

"What did you do?" said Gay. Her mind felt perfectly blank.

Sylvia was looking quite pleased.

"I just waited till he'd gone along to his bath. Of course he'd left his keys on the dressing-table — men always do — and the paper was in his despatch-box, just like the man said it would be, so I got it quite easily."

"Sylvia — what *are* you talking about? Francis — you took a paper out of Francis' despatch-box?"

"Oh, no," said Sylvia in a tone of surprise — "not Francis."

Gay wouldn't have believed that she could feel worse, but she did.

"You stole a paper from someone else. If it wasn't Francis, who was it?"

"The Home Secretary man — at least, I think that's what he is. He's quite nice looking, but he's got such an ugly name — Biffington — Buffington-Billington — one of those names, you know."

"I suppose you mean Mr Lushington?"

Sylvia brightened.

"Darling, you're so clever about names. Yes, Lushington. And his wife's sister is married to Binks."

"Binks?"

"Binks Wessex-Gardner — he is Buffo's brother. They were all staying with the Wessex-Gardners, and so were we. Darling, they've got the most lovely place. And you never saw anything like her clothes — too *too* of course, but *dreams*. She had an evening dress all white and gold patent leather —"

"What was this paper you stole?" said Gay.

Sylvia winced.

"Oh, that's a horrid word!"

"It's a horrid thing. What paper was it?"

Sylvia stared.

"I haven't the least idea."

"What did it look like? You must know that."

"Oh, yes, he told me. He said it would be a sort of list on a piece of paper — what do they call that big sort of paper?"

Gay's eyes danced for a moment.

"Do you mean foolscap?"

"Yes, that's it! And there wasn't any printing on it — just a lot of writing and a list of names — in one of those long envelopes. And he said I was to take the envelope just as it was, after I'd looked inside to see if it was the right one, and he said I was to put a plain envelope there instead."

Gay gave a horrified gasp.

"Sylvia!"

"I did it very well," said Sylvia with innocent pride.

"You put a plain envelope there instead?"

Sylvia nodded.

"Yes, he told me to — he said to take one off Francis' table, and he told me what size, and he said to put some paper inside it to make it look all right, and I did."

"Sylvia — you said you had to look inside the envelope you took to make sure it was the right one?"

"Yes, and I did. I was ever so quick."

"What were you to look for?"

Sylvia's white brow wrinkled.

"I keep forgetting the word — such a funny one — something to do with shoes —"

Gay said sharply, "Nonsense, Sylly!"

"Oh, but it was — not English ones — those French wooden things —"

"*Sabots?*"

Sylvia's brow relaxed.

"Yes, that was it — that's what I had to look for. He said it would be there, right on top, and it was — sabotage."

"What did you do with it?" said Gay in a tired voice.

"I did exactly what he said. I didn't make any mistakes. I put the envelope in my bag. And after dinner we were in the winter garden and they were playing cards, and what I was to do was to walk down

22

the drive and keep close to the bushes on the left, so I did. I had a fur wrap of course, and when I got about half way down someone flashed a light on me and I stopped, and I said, 'Who is it?' like he told me to, so as to be quite sure of not making a mistake and giving it to the wrong person. And he said, 'Mr Zero,' like he said he would, so then I gave him the envelope."

"Did you see him?"

Sylvia shook her head.

"Oh, no — it was dark. Besides, he didn't come out of the bushes. He just put out a hand and took the envelope. And then he gave me another with the money in it, and I ran back as fast as I could."

Gay still had the two pieces of newspaper in her left hand. She looked at them now, her mind quite dark, quite helpless. "Same time — same place — same money —" She read the words aloud.

"What does it mean?" she said.

"It means he wants some more papers," said Sylvia.

CHAPTER
FOUR

Gay went to the window, wrestled with it, opened it, and stuck her head out into the foggy, frosty air. Sylvia was exactly like a jelly, a beautiful, bright, quivering jelly with plenty of sweet whipped cream round it. If you had to talk to her for any length of time, you began to feel as if you were sinking into the jelly and smothering there. The warm room, Marcia's fripperies, Sylvia's violet scent, and all that rose colour were suddenly too much for her. The carpet had begun to wave up and down in a horrid pink mist. She much preferred the January fog outside with the lights shining through it like orange moons, and the hard smell of soot and frost. It was cold though. Her head steadied and she drew back with a shiver, but she left an open handsbreath to keep the carpet steady.

Sylvia was doing her mouth with a pale pink lipstick. She gazed earnestly at her own reflection in the little platinum-backed mirror which belonged to the bag, and said in a plaintive voice,

"Darling — such a draught!"

"You made my head go round," said Gay. "You'd make anyone's head go round. Now, Sylvia, put all that rubbish away and listen!"

24

"Rubbish?" said Sylvia. She turned the mirror to show the diamond S on the back. "Why, it cost masses of money."

Gay pounced, removed the lipstick and mirror, put them into the grey suede bag, and shut it with a snap.

"Now, Sylvia, *listen*. You say you were told all about stealing this paper on the telephone, but here —" she put the blue-pencilled message down on Sylvia's knee, — "here it says, 'Same time — same place — same money.' What does that mean? It doesn't fit in. What time? What place?"

Sylvia looked at the torn piece of paper. Then she looked at Gay.

"Well, he wanted me to go there again, but I wouldn't."

"He wanted you to go *where?* Where had you gone?"

"Well, it was at Cole Lester, you know."

"You were at Cole Lester when the man rang you up about stealing the paper?"

Sylvia looked surprised.

"Oh, no, darling, that was in London, but we were just going down to Cole Lester, and he said to wait till it was dark and then go and walk in the yew alley. It's very old, you know, hundreds and hundreds of years, and it meets overhead, so that it's like being in a tunnel. I didn't like it very much, but I thought I'd better go, and when I got to the end he said, 'Is that you?' And I said, 'Yes, and please be quick,' because that sort of place always has spiders and earwigs in it, and he hurried up and told me how to get the paper."

"He was in the alley?"

"Oh, no, darling — outside. I was the one who was in the alley. He was outside. There's a sort of window, and we talked through it, all whispery. I didn't like it a bit, and Francis might have thought the most dreadful things, so when he wanted me to go again I wouldn't. And now he says he'll tell Francis I took the paper, and if he does, Francis will know about the five hundred pounds, and I don't know what he'll say."

Gay tried to keep her head.

"You say this person wants another paper. How do you know he does?"

Sylvia's eyes widened.

"Darling, he *told* me."

Gay put a hand on her shoulder — a firm and angry little hand.

"Sylly, I shall shake you in about half a minute. How many times have you talked to this man?"

Sylvia began to count on her fingers.

"There was the time he rang up — that was the first time. And there was the time I've been telling you about at Cole Lester, and the time I was just starting for Wellings. And then I took the paper, and gave it to him, and he gave me the money — I don't know if you count that."

"Count everything," said Gay. "That's four. Now what is five?"

"I suppose it was when he rang me up again."

"He rang you up again? Where?"

"In Bruton Street. And he said he wanted me to do something else, and I said I couldn't, and I thought I heard Francis coming, so I rang off. And he rang up next day, and the minute I heard his voice I hung up, and he went on ringing for ages, and I just let him. And then I got a big cut out of a paper, and it just said, 'Two hundred and fifty pounds reward.' And next day this bit of paper —" she touched the torn piece on her knee — "and today there was the other one to say he was going to tell Francis, and if he does, I shall die."

Gay took her hand away, walked to the window, stared blankly at the fog, and came back again.

"You'll have to tell Francis," she said.

Sylvia's colour failed suddenly and completely.

"He'll kill me," she said in a frightened whisper.

"Nonsense, Sylly!"

"He said he would."

"Francis said he'd kill you?"

Sylvia's eyes were terrified.

"No, no — the man — he said he'd kill me if I told Francis — and he would — he said he'd kill me if I even thought about telling Francis."

"When did he say all this?"

"I think it was last night," said Sylvia vaguely. "I didn't mean to listen, but he said I must. And we're going down to Cole Lester, and if I don't take him the papers, he'll tell Francis —"

"What papers does he want this time?" said Gay.

Sylvia looked at her with brimming eyes.

"The ones Francis keeps in the safe in his study," she said.

CHAPTER
FIVE

Algy Somers jumped out of the taxi, ran up the six
steps which led up to Miss Agatha Hardwicke's front
door, and rang the bell. Almost before it had finished
ringing the door opened and Gay appeared. That was
one of the nice things about Gay, she never kept you
waiting. If you said nine o'clock, nine o'clock it was.
Algy had bitter memories of girls to whom nine meant
anything this side of ten o'clock.

Gay said, "Hully, Algy!" ran down the steps, jumped
into the taxi, and settled herself, all in one quick flash.

Algy Somers was one of the very kind-hearted people
who helped to make life with Aunt Agatha endurable by
taking her out. The fact that she was wearing the same
old black dress in which she had dined and danced ever
since the parents had departed to Madeira was not to
interfere in any way with her enjoyment, neither did she
mean to lose a single minute of it. That was another
nice thing about Gay, she enjoyed everything so much.
Her eyes shone and her cheeks glowed as she turned to
Algy and enquired,

"Where are we going?"

Algy looked at her admiringly, and then looked away,
because he was a careful young man and girls were apt

to get wind in the head if looked at like that. Gay, of course, wasn't like other girls, but still you had to watch your step. He said,

"I'm awfully sorry about dinner. I had to stay over time. Carstairs had a lot of stuff he wanted typed — confidential stuff, you know, so I couldn't take it home and do it later."

Gay looked away. She looked straight out in front of her over the bonnet of the car and along the dark street. It was one of those quiet streets where the houses look as if everyone in them always went to bed at ten o'clock. She said in a small, vague voice,

"Mr Carstairs is Mr Lushington's private secretary, isn't he?"

Algy stared at her profile.

"Well, you ought to know that by now."

Gay laughed suddenly.

"If you'd been talking to the sort of person I've been talking to this afternoon, you wouldn't be sure you knew anything. I wouldn't have sworn to my own name by the time I got away. I hope you don't expect me to be bright and sparkling, because that sort of thing leaves you as dull as ditchwater."

Algy was going to say that she couldn't be dull if she tried, but he thought better of it. An ambitious young man who has hopes of a political career cannot be too careful. He had begun to find Gay a trifle unbalancing. He proceeded to steady himself by talking about the career.

"I think Carstairs is getting a bit reconciled to having me about," he said. "He's Lushington's right hand of course, and he's so appallingly efficient himself that he can't stand anyone who isn't a hundred per cent punctual, orderly, accurate, discreet, and all the rest of the official virtues. Brewster, who's been there ten years, is the model — a frightfully brainy chap, and knows the job from A to Z. Well, when I came in, and when Carstairs knew that I was a sort of umpteenth cousin of Lushington's, he naturally made up his mind that I was going to be completely useless, and it's only by keeping the nose on the grindstone in the most unremitting manner that I have managed to allay his foul suspicions. Do you know that I've only been late once in eighteen solid months?"

"*Marvellous!*" said Gay. "How do you do it?"

"Well, the once was quite early on, and Carstairs looked at me with a cold, penetrating eye and said in a voice like a north-east wind, 'This must not occur again, Somers.' And, my child, I saw to it that it didn't occur. Look here, I thought we'd dance — and then what about a spot of supper and a cabaret? They've got a marvellous show at the Ducks and Drakes."

"Lovely," said Gay.

The Ducks and Drakes had a very good floor. People were telling each other that it was the best floor in London. There was a new sort of cocktail, and a new coloured dancer — "Simply too marvellous, my dear — her boa-constrictor dance — well, no bones at all! *The most amazing thing!*" This being the case, the floor was, naturally, so crowded that for the most part you did not so much dance as oscillate gently to the strains of the latest swing tune.

30

Gay and Algy oscillated with the rest. A saxophone moaned like a wounded siren. The rhythm drummed and thrummed and beat its way through the commonplace melody. The most archaic sense of all awoke to it, thrilled to it, kept time to it. The soloist lifted up a nasal tenor and sang with swooning sweetness, "Heaven's in your arms, and I'm there."

When the music stopped they found two chairs and one of the little red and black striped tables. There were quite a lot of well known people in the room, and Algy was much gratified at being able to do showman.

"That's Mrs Parkington who broke the woman's altitude record the other day. They say she's an awfully good sort. And that's Parkington with her. They're the most devoted couple, but he never stops being sick in a plane, so she has to leave him behind — she says he unnerves her. And that's Jessie Lanklater, the new tap-dancer, and the man with her is Lew Levinsky who wrote the music of *Up She Goes Again*. And the woman with red hair who has just come in is Poppy Wessex-Gardner."

Gay pricked up her ears. She saw a very tall, very thin woman with flaming hair and flaming lipstick in a long sheath-like garment which looked as it if was made of sheet cooper. Strands of copper wire were wound about her arms from shoulder to wrist. Her open sandals disclosed orange toe-nails.

"Does she always dress like that?"

"Or more so," said Algy. "The little fat, bald man is the husband who provides the cash — masses, and masses, and masses of cash. And the fellow who looks as if he'd just bought us all at a jumble sale is one Danvers. I don't know anything about him except his name, and I don't want to."

"I shouldn't think you did."

"I don't. I say, there's Cyril Brewster, the chap I was telling you about. I don't know who the lovely he's talking to is, but she's something to write home about, isn't she?"

Mr Brewster was a thin, dark young man with a pince-nez and an earnest expression. Gay looked at him, and set him down as a bromide. Then she looked past him to a vision in blue and silver. She said,

"He's talking to my cousin, Sylvia Colesborough."

Algy gazed.

"I say — is she really your cousin?"

Gay laughed without quite knowing why. Why should you laugh when your best young man is quite obviously struck all of a heap by someone else? She laughed and said,

"I suppose she is."

"How do you mean, you suppose?"

Gay laughed again.

"Well, she and Marcia and I were at school together, and when we were pleased with each other we were cousins, and when we quarrelled we weren't. I think we had the same great-great-grandfather."

"Definitely a cousin," said Algy. "I say, she's marvellous — isn't she? Will you introduce me? I'd like to cut out Brewster, and I'd like to be able to say I'd danced with anything as marvellous as that."

32

Gay flew a little scarlet flag in either cheek, a little scarlet danger flag. She said in a small, meek voice,

"And what happens to me, darling? Do I practice being a wallflower, or do I dance with Cyril?"

"You dance with Cyril," said Algy firmly. Then he grinned, and with the grin went back to being the schoolboy of ten years ago. "Unless you'd rather be a wallflower. You'd be awfully decorative, but I don't suppose you've had enough practice to do it really well. I say, you don't mind, do you? I expect it did sound a bit curt, but I would like to dance with her — just once — just to say I'd done it."

"All right, you shall. She dances beautifully too, but your Cyril Brewster's got her for this one."

"Do you want to dance it?"

Gay shook her head.

"I'd rather look on, then we can catch them as soon as they stop. Besides, I want to talk to you."

Algy's eyes followed the blue and silver vision.

"She's wasted on Brewster," he said with regret. "He'll bore her."

Gay suppressed a giggle.

"He won't. The man doesn't live who can bore Sylvia."

Algy looked at her darkly.

"You don't know Brewster. He'd bore anyone, and he'd do it as perseveringly and efficiently as he does everything else."

"Then I'd rather be a wallflower," said Gay.

Algy smiled upon her kindly.

"Oh, no, you wouldn't. But I'll rescue you after one dance — I swear I will. Anyhow, he's quite an efficient dancer."

"Algy, I want to talk to you."

"All right, I'm here. What do you want to talk about?"

"I want to ask you something."

"All right, ask away, I haven't got a kingdom, but if I had one, you could have half of it. I can't say fairer than that."

And he hadn't meant to say that. It just slipped out. There was something about Gay sitting up rather straight and looking rather earnest that made it slip out. The blue and silver lovely was a godsend, because he mustn't, he really mustn't slip over the edge of being in love with Gay, and when she looked at him with something young and a little forlorn behind the sparkle in her eyes, the edge was dangerously near.

"Algy, what would you do if someone tried to blackmail you?"

"I should tell him to go to blazes," said Algy promptly.

Gay considered this. It seemed to her a simple and efficacious method, but it was no use commending it to Sylvia. She sighed and said,

"Suppose you couldn't — I mean, suppose you weren't like that — I mean some people can't tell people to go to blazes — they just can't."

Algy's agreeable features took on an expression of gravity.

34

"I think they had better try," he said. "And if they can't manage it themselves, I think they had better go to the police. After all, that's what the police are for, you know."

"That's all very well," said Gay, "but suppose the blackmailer wouldn't go to blazes, and you couldn't go to the police."

"Why couldn't you?" said Algy quickly.

Gay looked serious too.

"The thing you were being blackmailed about might be the sort of thing you couldn't go and chat about to a policeman."

Algy began to feel dreadfully perturbed.

"Look here, is this a hypothetical case, or is somebody blackmailing you?"

Gay flashed into brilliance. Her eyes sparkled, and the red flags danced in a brisk, angry breeze.

"What do you think I've done?"

"I didn't think you'd done anything."

"Well, you don't get blackmailed for nothing — do you?"

"I don't know — I've never tried."

"Nor have I!"

There was anger between them under the wordplay — quick cut and thrust of anger, quick unreasoning cut and thrust. It surprised them both. It surprised Gay so much that she caught her breath and said,

"We're quarrelling. I don't know why. We've never quarrelled before."

"It's never too late to mend." He looked at her with laughing eyes. "You're awfully funny to quarrel with."

35

"Funny?"

"Like a robin pecking."

"Robins are fierce. They fight like anything."

"All right, I'll be careful. Let's get back to the blackmailer. What does he want? It's absolutely fatal to start giving money. The horse-leech isn't in it — the more you give, the more he'll want, and the more he'll get. Seriously, Gay, if you know anyone who is being blackmailed, tell them that."

"It isn't money — he doesn't want money."

"What is it then?"

Gay's lively colour died. She looked uncertain, pale, frightened.

"I don't think I can tell you. It's something — it might be something dreadful."

"Gay!"

She jumped up. The music was stopping — just in time — just in time — just in time. For what had she been going to say? And why was it so dreadfully easy to say things to Algy? It scared her. She spoke a little breathlessly.

"Come along with me and meet Sylvia if you want to. She'll be snapped up in a second."

Sylvia looked surprised and pleased when Gay slipped a hand under her arm.

"Gay — *darling!* How did you get here?"

Gay's other hand indicated the slightly abashed Mr Somers.

"He brought me. He's one of the kind hearts, and it was his scout deed for the day. His name is Algy Somers, and as a reward he would like very much to dance with you. Algy — Lady Colesborough. He knows Francis — a little."

"I don't think —" began Sylvia. Then she met Algy's admiring gaze and wavered. "Mr Brewster — and then I'm dancing with Mr Wessex-Gardner —"

"I shouldn't," said Algy — "I really, really shouldn't. I know seventeen women in London who are crippled for life because they were reckless enough to dance with him. He's a confirmed toe-treader and ankle-kicker. He's known at his club as the Bonesetter's Friend. Brewster, this is Miss Gay Hardwicke, and she will be kind enough to give you the next dance if you ask her very nicely." He gazed at Sylvia, offered her his arm, and when after a moment of indecision she took it, he bore her away in triumph, leaving behind him a darkly annoyed Mr Brewster, and Gay Hardwicke, who smiled prettily and had a horrid little jabbing pain in her mind.

Cyril Brewster was a polite young man. He said, "May I have the pleasure?" and Gay said, "Yes," and the music struck up again and they danced.

It was a very efficient performance on Mr Brewster's part, but it lacked thrill. There was plenty of swing in the music, but what is the good of swing in the music if there isn't any swing in your partner? Gay caught a glimpse of Sylvia floating in Algy's arms. Sylvia really did float — like a cloud, like a wave, like a leaf in the wind.

The crooner lifted up his voice and crooned:

"You're mine this minute.
That's all that's in it

and there's no limit
To my ecstasy."

Cyril Brewster said, in the voice which indicated that a remark has been repeated for the second time,

"Have you known Lady Colesborough for long?"

"I'm so sorry," said Gay — "I was thinking about something else. What did you say?"

Mr Brewster repeated his remark for the third time — patiently.

"I said, 'Have you known Lady Colesborough for long?'"

"Twenty years," said Gay, and then giggled because he looked as if he didn't believe her. "She's a cousin, you know, and we bit each other in the nursery — at least I did the biting and Sylvia did the kissing and making friends afterwards."

"She must have been a lovely child," said Cyril Brewster earnestly.

"Everyone says so. I expect that was why I bit."

Cyril put his pince-nez straight. He did this constantly, but it never stayed put.

"I have only met her three times," he said. "I think she is extremely beautiful."

"Everyone thinks so," said Gay firmly.

"It is unusual to find anyone with so many attractions. As a rule there is something lacking, but Lady Colesborough has everything. Of course, I do not know her well enough to speak of anything but externals. If it is possible to judge by those, her disposition should be as charming as her face."

"She has a very amiable disposition," said Gay.

Algy was perfectly right. Brewster was a most efficient bore, and, like all bores, there was no stopping him. He wanted to talk about Sylvia, and he intended to talk about Sylvia. He went on talking about Sylvia.

"The first time I met her was not really a meeting at all. She was walking with Mrs Wessex-Gardner, and I bowed — to Mrs Wessex-Gardner. And the second time she was also walking in the park —"

"With Mrs Wessex-Gardner?"

"No — she was alone, so of course I couldn't bow. But tonight Mrs Wessex-Gardner very kindly asked me to join her party, and I was introduced to her. As you are her cousin, perhaps you will tell me a little more about her. Is she a widow?"

"Certainly not. She's only been married for a year."

"And her husband?"

"He is Sir Francis Colesborough, because his father made a lot of money in — well, I think it was timber — and gave away parks, and playgrounds, and things, so they made him a baronet. He bought a most lovely old place called Cole Lester. I believe he bought it because of the name being like his own, and of course it belongs to Francis now."

"I see," said Cyril. "And do they live there a good deal?"

"I don't think so. Sylvia likes London. She was brought up in the country, you know, so she's had enough of it. Francis seems to go away a lot on business."

"Ah, yes, — I suppose he would." He went on talking about Sylvia and asking questions. The crooner's voice came through again:

> "I'm feeling lazy.
> My mind's all hazy
> Because I'm crazy
> With my ecstasy."

CHAPTER
SIX

It was rather a disappointing evening, because Algy when he came back would do nothing but talk about Sylvia too. Even in the taxi going home he was still saying how lovely she was. And of course it was all quite true. Sylvia was lovely, and that was all there was about it. And Gay wasn't lovely at all, and no one would ever feel rewarded by winning a dance from her. She wasn't a bad little thing, and she had her points of course — good hair, and — yes, really good eyes — and a good colour too, though nowadays when everyone could put it on that didn't go for so much — and good teeth — oh, yes, really good teeth. Gay would stick up for Gay on all these points, but what was the good if Algy had no eyes for anyone but Sylvia?

She caught a glimpse of herself in the glass at the side of the taxi, and saw a plain little Gay with no colour at all and the sparkle gone from her eyes. They were very nearly home, and she was glad.

She turned, and saw Algy beside her like a shadow. The light that had showed her her own face was gone. They were in Hunt Street again and it was fast asleep, not a light in any one of the crowded houses, and the street-lamps few and dim and far between. Miss Hardwicke's house was No. 36.

The taxi drew up. Algy paid it off and came up the steps with Gay. He said,

"I'll walk home. I'm short of fresh air and exercise."

Gay said nothing. She was looking in her bag for the latchkey. It was a black velvet bag with a cut steel handle, and it had belonged to Aunt Henrietta, who was an aunt of Aunt Agatha's, and the velvet had lasted all those years and never worn out. It wasn't even shabby. Other things didn't wear so well — being friends, and — and liking people —

Gay found her key and shut the bag again, but she didn't put the key in the lock. She just stood there, and Algy just stood there. The hooded porch was over them, and the street was dark. There was no sound at all — no sound. Neither of them moved. Neither of them spoke for a long time. Then Gay lifted the key and put it into the lock, and as she did that, Algy's hand came past her shoulder and closed down over her hand and over the key, and Gay's hand shook. Algy said, "Gay —" in an odd muffled voice, and Gay turned the key, pushed the door open, and ran in. She stood just inside with the hall light shining behind her, and said in a bright, clear voice, "Night, Algy. Thanks ever so much," and sent the door to with a bang that brought Aunt Agatha out in a dressing-gown and a cap rather like a string shopping-bag to enquire what sort of hour of the night Gay thought it was, and what did she think she was going to be like next day.

Gay went on up to her room and shut the door with a sense of escape. She was rather out of breath, and her cheeks were as hot as if she had been scorching them over a fire, but her hand was cold, as cold as if it had been in ice-cold water. She was angrier with herself than she had ever been in all her life before. What did she think she was doing, turning hot and cold and going all dithery inside just because Algy Somers had grabbed her hand like that? Only he hadn't grabbed it. His hand had come down upon hers and stayed there. Gay spoke very fiercely to herself. "You just get into bed as quick as you can and take a book and read till your eyes pop out. And don't you dare to think about Algy again tonight — and there's not so much of tonight left either."

Algy Somers walked home through a number of dark, quiet by-ways. If some parts of London never go to bed, there are others which sleep very soundly indeed. Algy's footsteps had only their own echo for company, and as he walked he was wondering what had happened to him. He hadn't known that he was going to take Gay's hand like that. Something had come up between them as they stood together in the dark porch, and before he knew what he was going to do his hand had closed on hers. The feel of that little hand, and the way it shook under his, was tingling in him still. What he ought to be feeling was relief, because if Gay hadn't pulled away like that and run into the house, there was really no saying what he might have said or done. He might have said anything, he might have committed himself quite hopelessly, and instead of being grateful for a most providential interruption he was raging because Gay had run away from him. And why? That was what he wanted to know. Why had her hand been all shaky under his, and why had she run away? Was she angry with him, or was she afraid, or . . . ?

It was some time after this that he came to with a start and realized that he hadn't the very faintest idea where he was. He didn't know where he was, and he didn't even know how long it had taken him to get there. It took him quite a long time to get home.

Sylvia Colesborough heard the wall-clock in her sitting-room strike three as she came up the stair. It was the very latest thing in clocks, a bright stretch of glass with the numerals raised in mirror points, and the hands a delicate fretwork of stainless steel. Everything in the room was new and bright, and, to Sylvia's taste, very, very beautiful. She hated things that were old, or partly worn, or out of fashion. She had grown up amongst things like that and she hated them. Everything in her own sitting-room and in the bedroom next door to it was quite, quite new.

She went into the bedroom and began to undress, moving to and fro with her slow, invariable grace. Sylvia never hurried. She put everything away as she took it off. It had never occurred to her to let her maid sit up for her when she was going to be late. She liked to come alone into her lovely room and go softly to and fro without feeling that there was any need to hurry. The room made a perfect setting for her. The colours in it were all the colours of ice — pale green and blue, and all the shades between. The bed, a classically shaped couch, the dressing-table, and the stool that belonged to it were all made of heavy glass, semi-opaque and with a bluish tinge, but there was bright glass too — brightly faceted glass in the wreath about a mirror, in the clustered ceiling lights, and mirror glass everywhere so that as she moved Sylvia could see herself reflected from every side. Every looking-glass panel was a door. Behind one the bathroom, all pale green glass. Behind the others Sylvia's many lovely dresses, her hats, her shoes, her filmy, delicate underwear. Sylvia loved her mirrors — loved to see her own reflection come and go, loved the light, the pale colours, and the dazzling brilliance of it all. She loved it most when Francis was away.

It wasn't that she disliked Francis — she was much too amiable to do that. Had he not given her all these beautiful things? If it were not for Francis she would still be penniless Sylvia Thrale, living with a widowed mother in a small provincial town and being made love to by curates and bank clerks. She shuddered at the thought that she might have married one of them. It was Francis who had saved her from this, and since he was her husband and she had promised to be fond of him, in church and with six bridesmaids and a large congregation all listening to her, it followed as a matter of course that she *was* fond of Francis. But he was away a lot, and life was much, much pleasanter when he was away — much, much pleasanter.

Sylvia put on a white embroidered chiffon nightdress and sat down on the edge of her wide, low bed to take off her slippers. As the second slipper dropped, the telephone bell rang sharply. The instrument stood on a heavy glass pedestal beside the bed and was masked by the translucent figure of a dancer with outspread skirts.

She got into bed, and when the bell rang a second time she took up the receiver and put it to her ear. It was silly of her heart to beat so fast, because nobody in the world would ring her up at this hour except Francis — nobody in the whole world. But Francis might — Francis sometimes did when he was away like this.

A man's voice said, "Hullo!" It sounded a long way off. Francis was a long way off. He was somewhere abroad, she wasn't quite sure where. Francis very seldom told her where he went to on his business journeys.

The faraway voice said, "Hullo!" again.

Sylvia said, "Who's there?" And the voice said, "Mr Zero."

Gay would have hung up in a rage, but Sylvia wasn't Gay Hardwicke. The receiver shook, and her hand shook, and her heart shook too. She said,

"I can't talk to you — I really can't. Please, *please* go away."

Mr Zero laughed. He had an odd, cold laugh which frightened Sylvia extremely. He said,

"Neither of us is going away until we've got our little bit of business fixed up. I'm a martyr to business, and if you don't want to be a martyr too, and a slaughtered martyr at that, you'll stay just where you are and listen to me until I say you can hang up."

Sylvia was puzzled to the point of forgetting to be frightened. In a tone of pure bewilderment she said,

"I don't know what you mean."

Mr Zero laughed again.

"Dear me — I was forgetting that I must use words of one syllable! Very, very stupid of me. Please accept my apologies. And now to business. If you ring off before I've finished with you, I shall write and tell your husband about the paper you took last week. Is that quite clear?"

"*No!*" said Sylvia with a gasp. "Oh, no — you wouldn't! I mean, you won't!"

"Not if you do as you're told. And the first thing is, you are not to hang up until I say you can."

Sylvia felt a slight relief. If that was all, she could do that. She pulled up a pale blue sheet and a pale green blanket and settled herself against the pillows that matched them. If she had got to talk to this horrible man she might as well be comfortable.

Mr Zero was speaking, still in that faraway voice.

"I will put everything very simply. As far as possible there shall only be words of one syllable. If I go into two or three syllables, put a wet towel round your head and do your best to understand me."

"But it would spoil my wave," said Sylvia in a tone of sincere protest.

"Well, well, I don't insist upon the towel. Now listen to me! Is your husband away?"

"Oh, yes."

"When does he come back?"

"Tomorrow — at least I think so."

"He takes his keys with him of course?"

"Oh, yes."

"Where does he keep them when he is at home? No, I can tell you that — he has them on a chain in his trouser pocket and changes them over when he changes his clothes. A very careful person. What I don't know, and what I want you to tell me is what he does with them at night. Does he leave them on his dressing-table?"

Sylvia had almost stopped being frightened. This was quite easy to answer.

"Only when he goes to his bath," she said.

"And the bathroom opens out of his dressing-room?"

Sylvia drew in her breath in surprise.

"How do you know that?"

Mr Zero laughed. She did so wish that he wouldn't laugh.

"Never mind — it does, doesn't it? Is he one of the people who enjoy a good long, lingering bath? Could you do anything about the keys then?"

"Oh, no — his man is there."

"Always?"

"Oh, yes, always."

"Are you telling the truth?" said Mr Zero.

Sylvia was very much affronted. She drew herself up against her pillow and said,

"I always tell the truth."

She heard that horrid laugh again.

"*Always?*"

"Except when I *can't.*"

"I see. And you're sure this isn't one of those times?"

He had puzzled her again.

"I don't know what you mean."

"No — my fault — sorry. Back to the infant class again. Your husband's man stays in the dressing-room all the time?"

"Oh, yes."

"Well, what happens at night? What does he do with the keys then?"

"He puts them under his pillow."

Mr Zero said briskly,

"A very prudent habit. And is he a sound sleeper?"

"Oh, yes, very."

"Then it is all quite easy. You wait till he is asleep, you take the keys from under the pillow, and you come downstairs and open the left-hand dining-room window — the one on your own left as you come into the room. You will give me the keys out of the window."

"Oh no — I couldn't!"

"You will give me the keys, and you will wait till I give them back to you. I shall only be a few minutes. Then I will give them to you again, and you will put them back under your husband's pillow. It is all as simple as eating bread and milk. I shall be waiting by the dining-room window from one to two tomorrow night, and you will bring me the keys then."

"I don't think I can," said Sylvia in a weak and yielding voice.

CHAPTER
SEVEN

Mr Montagu Lushington looked up at the sound of the opening door. He was sitting at a writing-table in the study of his own house. He was rather a handsome man with a noticeable crop of grey hair, and hazel eyes which could be shrewd, dreamy, or restless. They were restless now. He drummed with his fingers on the arm of his chair and said,

"Come in and shut the door, Algy."

Algy Somers wondered what he had done. There had been signs of dirty weather all the week, but this had the appearance of a gale warning to all coasts.

"Sit down," said Mr Lushington.

Algy began to wonder if he was going to get the sack. Only if Monty was going to sack him, would he ask him to sit down? He said,

"Yes, sir?"

Mr Lushington leaned back. The movement was an impatient one.

"What sort of memory have you got, Algy?"

Dismay invaded Algy's mind. What had he forgotten? He said modestly,

"Oh, I don't know — pretty fair as a rule. I hope I haven't been forgetting anything, sir."

Mr Lushington frowned.

"That remains to be seen. I want you to cast your mind back to last Saturday."

Algy's mind went back to a very pleasant evening spent with Miss Gay Hardwicke. He had no difficulty in recalling the agreeable details, but it did not seem at all likely that they would interest Monty. He said,

"Saturday, sir?"

"Last Saturday I went away for the week-end. I went down to Wellings to stay with the Wessex-Gardners, and just before I started a special messenger turned up with a memorandum which I had asked for from the Intelligence. Now take over and tell me exactly what happened. Who saw the messenger?"

"Mr Carstairs saw him, sir."

"I want you to go over the whole thing — I want every detail."

"Mr Carstairs and I were in here. Mr Carstairs had just come down from seeing you. Parkinson came in and said there was a messenger, and Carstairs — Mr Carstairs — went to the door and took the letter. He was going up with it, but the telephone bell rang, and it was someone for him, so he told me to take the letter."

Mr Lushington drummed with his fingers.

"One moment, one moment. Were you and Carstairs alone? Where was Brewster?"

"Oh, he was somewhere around."

"Can't you be accurate? What on earth do you mean by somewhere around?"

"Well, he was in the offing, don't you know, sir? Nose to the grindstone and all that sort of thing."

"You mean he was in this room?"

"Oh, yes — definitely."

"But he didn't handle the letter?"

"Oh, no, sir."

"Did you see Carstairs take the letter from the messenger?"

Algy considered for a moment.

"Well, I heard him say, 'Mr Lushington is upstairs. I will take it up to him.' And I heard the man say, 'Thank you, sir.' And then Mr Carstairs came back into the room with the envelope in his hand, and the telephone bell rang, and he told me to take it up to you, and I did."

"No one else touched it?"

"No one."

"And you came straight up with it? It wasn't out of your hand at all?"

"Oh, no, sir."

Montagu Lushington said,

"Very well then — go on."

Algy restrained an expression of surprise.

"But you know all the rest, sir. You were in your dressing-room, and I put the envelope down on the table."

Mr Lushington nodded.

"Go on. I have my own recollection of what happened, but I want yours — every detail, please."

"You were packing your suit-case, sir. It was on the bed, and so was your despatch-box. They were both open. You put a pair of socks into the suit-case, and then you took up the envelope and said, 'What's this?'

And I said, 'Just come round by messenger from the Intelligence. Mr Carstairs told me to bring it up.' And you said, 'Yes, yes — I asked them to let me have it,' and you picked it up, and put it in on the top of your despatch-box, and locked the case, and put the keys back in your pocket. And you said that was all, and I cleared out."

"You saw me put the envelope in the despatch-case and lock it away?"

"Yes, sir."

There was a silence. Montagu Lushington looked long and shrewdly at his young cousin. In the end he said,

"Did you notice how the letter was addressed?"

What in the name of fortune did this mean? Algy tried to keep surprise out of his voice as he said,

"No — I didn't look at it, I'm afraid. Carstairs — Mr Carstairs — gave it to me. He said it was the sabotage memorandum you had asked for from the Intelligence, and told me to take it up to you. I never thought of looking at it."

Mr Lushington said, "I see. You didn't notice the envelope at all? Now what I want you to tell me is this. You put the envelope down on the table, and I picked it up and put it away in my despatch-case. Think before you speak, please. Did you see me look at it or read the address?"

"I don't think I did."

"You don't think — that's not good enough. Can't you be more exact than that?"

"I'm afraid I can't, sir. I wasn't taking very much notice. You see, I'd given you the envelope, so I wasn't thinking about it any more." He paused, and then went on again. "I think you just picked it up and put it into your despatch-box. I don't think you looked at it."

Mr Lushington pushed back his chair.

"I expect you are wondering what this is all about."

"It's not my business to wonder, is it, sir?"

Mr Lushington frowned.

"It may be. I am going to talk to you in confidence, Algy. You are a member of my family as well as a member of my staff, and I wish to make it quite clear that what I am saying is not to go any farther. To begin with, the papers which you brought me have disappeared. I went down to the Wessex-Gardners, as you know, and I did not open my despatch-case until round about midnight, when I went up to my room for the night. When I did open it, there was a plain manila envelope right on top of the other papers. It bore no address, and there was a sheet of blank foolscap inside. That is why I asked whether you had noticed the address on the envelope you brought me."

"But, sir —"

"Wait! My keys had never been out of my possession. I had a bath before dinner, and they were on the dressing-table with my watch and note-case, but the bathroom had a communicating door, and I am pretty sure that it was ajar. Besides — and here is the point — how could anyone at the Wessex-Gardners' have known that I should have this memorandum in my possession? The party was quite a small one — myself and my wife, the Colesboroughs, and the Bingham Wessex-Gardners. Bingham, as you probably know, married my wife's sister Constance. It was therefore something in the nature of a family party, but I also wished to take the opportunities it would afford of some quite informal conversations with Beaufort Wessex-Gardner and Francis Colesborough. They are both undertaking very large government contracts. This question of sabotage would affect them."

Algy hesitated, and risked a question.

"Was the memorandum very important?"

Mr Lushington drummed on the arm of his chair.

"Oh, the skies won't fall. There have been, as you know, a certain number of acts of sabotage. There have been allusions in the Press, and there have been questions in the House. There has been some uneasiness, and a general tightening up of precautionary measures. Then the Foreign Office Intelligence came along with the theory of an organization directed from abroad and with very wide ramifications." He paused. Algy was aware of scrutiny.

Mr Lushington went on speaking.

"Colonel Garratt is convinced that such an organization exists. He believes that it has plans for sabotage on a large scale. If this country were faced with a sudden emergency, these plans would be brought into operation. He has compiled a list of suspected agents, and was very anxious that I should sanction a general round up. I wished to think the matter over, and asked to be furnished with a memorandum and a list of the suspected persons before the week-end. The envelope delivered to Carstairs contained this information. It came from Colonel Garratt through our own people, and I am not excluding the possibility of a leakage, but it is sufficiently obvious that there would have been no need to steal the papers if the information had already been obtained from either of the departments concerned. When I say that the messenger is above suspicion, I have regard not only to his character and length of service, but to the fact that it is incredible that he would have risked substituting a blank envelope for the one addressed to me, when all that he had to do was to allow the enclosures to be copied or photographed. He could not possibly have anticipated that neither Carstairs, nor you, nor I myself would not immediately examine the envelope and detect the fraud. Now, Algy, I am coming to the point. The papers were stolen a week ago. I am advised that a raid would not be likely to produce sufficient evidence to justify itself. Whoever had an interest in acquiring the papers has therefore probably achieved his end. He has found out which of his agents are under suspicion. He has been able to warn them, and he will probably now replace them by others. We shall have to begin all over again. As I said before, the skies won't fall, but what matters to me is the suggestion that the papers were stolen here in my own house."

Algy felt exactly as if someone had poured about half a pint of cold water down the back of his neck, because — well, after all — hang it all — what was Monty saying?

56

He said aloud, "Yes, sir?" and was rather proud of the fact that the words came out in quite an ordinary tone.

"It has been suggested to me —" this was Monty on the high horse of offence — "it has been suggested that it would have been far more credible that an attempt to steal the papers should be made here, where the fact that I was expecting them was known, and their nature if not known was at least guessed at, rather than at Wellings, where no one could reasonably be supposed to have any information on the subject."

Algy had been thinking. His thoughts made a clear and very unpleasant pattern. He wanted to get up, to shout out the fury and anger which filled him. But he did not do either of these things. He sat quite still, and he said quietly,

"That puts it on me."

"That is why I am talking to you like this," said Montagu Lushington. "When you say that this puts it on you, you are perhaps exaggerating. Four people handled the envelope in this house —"

"Four?"

Mr Lushington inclined his head.

"The messenger — Carstairs — you, Algy — and I. The messenger really is above suspicion. Our own people swear to him. There remain Carstairs, whom I am prepared to swear to, and you, Algy, and myself. If I could remember reading the address upon the envelope I should be able to clear you, and in doing so I should prove, no doubt to some people's satisfaction, that I had abstracted the papers myself."

Algy looked across the table. His pleasant face had taken on the most unwontedly stern expression. He looked as he would not look, except under stress, for a dozen years at least. He said, still in that quiet voice,

"It does come back to me, you see. Do I have to say that I didn't do it, sir?"

He got the shrewd look again. Montagu Lushington said,

"Not to me, Algy."

CHAPTER
EIGHT

Algy Somers was dining out. He was dining with the Giles Westgates. Giles was his very good friend, and Linda was a cousin — one of the many cousins who bloomed, sprouted, and climbed on a highly prolific family tree. Linda and Giles knew everyone, went everywhere, and did everything. They probably knew all about the papers that had gone missing at the Wessex-Gardners' — the "all" not to be read to include criminal knowledge, but merely an expert collection of every scrap of fact and gossip on the subject. This being so, Algy had serious thoughts of getting the man at his rooms to ring up and say that he was dead. No lesser excuse would be any good, and Barker would do it awfully well — "Mr Somers' compliments, and he is very sorry indeed to inconvenience your table, madam, but he is unavoidably prevented from joining you tonight owing to his sudden decease." The dark melancholy of Barker's voice was made for messages like this, and wasted, lamentably wasted, on orders for groceries and fish.

Algy turned on his bath, and reflected that this was one of the most unpleasant days he had ever spent. The fog outside was nothing to the fog within. In this fog of suspicion, which didn't amount to accusation and would never amount to accusation, he had endured the long humiliating hours of a long humiliating day. He brought himself to realize that the future now promised an indefinite number of similar days. The Home Secretary had asked for an important memorandum on sabotage, and it had gone missing. Algy Somers was the person who had had by far the best opportunity of taking it. This was a quite insane, quite incontrovertible proposition. And there they were. And there he was. There was no evidence of course. Nobody would quite accuse him, nobody would quite believe him. There would be a whisper that would pursue him wherever he went and whatever he did. It would be prefaced by a vague "They say," or a hearty "Of course, I don't believe it, but —" and it would slide by insidious degrees from damaging into damning him. And only twenty-four hours ago he had been trying hard to remember that a young man with the ball at his foot had better put off thinking about marriage for another half dozen years or so. Well, there was no ball at his foot now, and nothing to offer Gay Hardwicke or any other girl. Monty would stand by him — Monty had behaved uncommon well — but the fact that he was a relation put them both in an awkward position. It would have been much easier, for instance, for Monty to stand up for Brewster.

Algy got into his bath, and considered with bitterness that Brewster had all the luck. Why couldn't it have been Brewster who had been told to take that damnable envelope up to Monty? A bit hard on

Brewster perhaps, but on the other hand imagination really boggled at the idea of anyone suspecting Brewster. He tried to picture him under suspicion and failed. Brewster was the perfect assistant secretary, the industrious apprentice, the human encyclopedia. No good bothering about Brewster. This was the affair of Algy Somers. What was Algy Somers going to do about it? See his good name and his prospects die a slow death from poison? Well then, what about it? The answer came to him vigorous and clear — "I've damn well got to find out who took those papers."

He ceased to lie supine in the gratifyingly hot water. You didn't expose villainy by lying in a hot bath — you girded yourself for the fray, and you went out and looked for the fellow who had really done the deed.

Algy proceeded to gird himself. He didn't know where he was going to look, but it occurred to him that Linda's dinner table wasn't at all a bad place to begin, because what he wanted to do was to listen to the voice of scandal. About the Wessex-Gardners, and the Wessex-Gardners' house-party.

He ran through the guests in his own mind. Monty had been a bit stiff over telling him about them, but had stood and delivered like a man in the end.

Beaufort and Poppy Wessex-Gardner. The host and hostess. He was the little man with the bald head at the Ducks and Drakes. Insignificant physically and no use socially, but a bulging forehead and probably a great brain. Anyhow he had made masses of money, and was now going to build aeroplanes for the government. They called him Buffo. Sabotage might interest him.

Poppy? Amazing clothes, bizarre make-up, moderate personal attractions, age very difficult to tell — somewhere between thirty-five and forty-five. Nothing to suggest whether she was or could be interested in anything or anyone except herself.

Another lot of Wessex-Gardners. Bingham and Constance. Man known as Binks. In business with his brother, but definitely a lesser light. Very good bridge-player. Constance — Maud Lushington's sister. Vague recollections of having met her — vague recollections of her being even more like a horse than Maud. It didn't seem possible, but the equine impression very strong.

Francis Colesborough and the lovely Sylvia. A peach of peaches. Quite, quite negligible in the affair of Algy Somers. She wouldn't even know what sabotage was, bless her.

He turned reluctantly to a less radiant image. Francis Colesborough. Very well set up, very well preserved. One of your forceful, industry-building fellows. Second generation of self-made family — timber, steel. Lots of irons in the fire. Lots of money. Easy, pleasant, reasonably good at all the things people are good at. Highly efficient, and full of government contracts. Just a trifle aloof.

Monty and Maud. Irreverence toyed with a fantasy of Maud abstracting Monty's papers. Algy had no deep affection for his cousin Maud by marriage — too much nose; too much upper lip; too many teeth; far, far too many bony ridges in front. Ungrateful of Algy, because Maud had quite an affection for him and always spoke of him as "my husband's young cousin." He sometimes wondered what would happen when he passed the thirty mark, and the thirty-five, and the forty. Would he become "my husband's middle-aged cousin" — and at what moment? Digressions apart, Monty and Maud were off the map. What remained not promising at all. Buffo, Poppy, Binks, Constance, Francis Colesborough, and the lovely Sylvia. It was really extremely difficult to imagine any of them pinching a government memorandum out of Monty's despatch-case with Monty next door having a bath. Worse than difficult — farcical. Well, when there are no probables you must take a possible, and if there aren't any possibles, you must work through the improbables, and may even end up with an impossible.

He stood frowning into the glass as he dealt with his tie. He was good at ties, and it came out well. Faint memories of some historic character who took particular pains over a toilet for the scaffold flitted through the hinterland of his mind. They were presently supplemented by the refrain of a ballad about the gentleman called Gilderoy:

"Sae rantingly, sae wantonly.
Sae dauntingly gae'd he.
He played a spring and danced it round
Beneath the gallows tree."

— the sort of thing that *would* come into your head at this sort of moment.

63

He buttoned his waistcoat and slipped his arms into his coat. With his hands at the lapels he surveyed the result. Not too bad. "Sae rantingly, sae wantonly —" There was the dashed thing again, and he couldn't even remember how he came to know it. He turned, and was aware of the light glancing oddly across the tail of his coat. The excellent Barker had furnished the room with a nice fumed oak suite. The wardrobe sported a long strip of mirror glass upon its door. Algy was always afraid that the weight of it would bring the whole thing over, but for the moment it stood firm. The glass showed a bulge in the left-hand tail where no bulge should be — something in the pocket. But there oughtn't to be anything in the pocket. He would never dream of putting anything there. People did of course — the cigarette-case. He knew a man who harboured a handkerchief — a most slovenly habit. But this wasn't a cigarette-case, and it certainly wasn't a handkerchief. It was stiff, and it crackled — paper — thickish paper. He drew it out, and beheld a manila envelope doubled up, folded neatly. He unfolded it, laid it flat. It was an official envelope, and it bore an official address:

The Rt. Hon'ble. Montagu Lushington.

The words dazzled, the words swam before Algy's horrified eyes. Because he had handled this envelope before. He had taken it from Carstairs at the study door and gone up to Monty's room and put it down on Monty's dressing-table. He hadn't looked at the address. He hadn't consciously looked at the envelope.

But now that he had it in his hand again, he knew that he had noticed the blot in the left-hand corner — a round blob of a blot which had dried very thick, and black, and shiny. This was undoubtedly Monty's envelope — the stolen envelope. And someone had planted it on him. Someone must have planted it on him at the Ducks and Drakes last night.

He stared at it. Why? Rather crass attempt to deepen suspicion? Or rather subtle attempt to put the wind up him? Other possibilities . . . Too many possibilities . . .

He turned the envelope over, and the flap hung loose. He lifted it and looked inside.

The envelope was empty.

CHAPTER
NINE

Giles and Linda Westgate lived in a flat which consisted of one large room and several darkish cupboards euphemistically labelled bedroom No. 1, bedroom No. 2, kitchen, and bathroom. Linda had done her best by painting each one a different colour and in the brightest possible shade. Her cupboard was a brilliant jade, Giles' canary-yellow, the bathroom emerald, and the kitchen a cheerful orange. The large room she had left alone. It had cream walls, a parquet floor, and no furniture except piles of cushions, a collapsible table, and a dozen chromium-plated chairs. Their brittle, angular brightness reminded Algy of some insect's legs — grasshopper, dragonfly, mantis.

Linda furnished her room with people. There were eight of them for dinner, and a crowd afterwards. She wore scarlet velvet, which went very well with her cream skin and her cream walls. She had black hair which never stayed where it was put, and dancing eyes with a dark, malicious sparkle in them — a vivid creature, decorative and talkative as a parrot and quite as indiscreet. Giles, a budding barrister, talked nearly as much as she did, and could be witty. They had a great many friends, and spared none of them.

Algy, coming into the room, was aware of a sudden silence which seemed so abnormal in any room of Linda's as to make him positive that they had been talking about him. If he flinched he contrived not to show it, and in a moment Linda was hanging on his arm and chattering at him.

"Algy darling, we were talking about you. Didn't you hear us all stop dead?" (Clever to take the bull by the horns like that.) "Would you like to know what we were saying?"

Algy said, "Very much." But he thought he knew already, and he thought that he wouldn't be very likely to hear the truth, or to like it if he did.

There were four people there besides the Westgates. Two of them laughed, and two made rather a lamentable failure of an attempt to appear quite easy and comfortable. Algy looked round, said how do you do to the friend of Linda's who had been asked to balance a friend of Giles' — pretty girl with red hair; dark young man with a superiority complex — and to James and Mary Craster, whom he liked. It was James and Mary who had been embarrassed, and the other two who had laughed.

"And what were you saying about me?" he said, and saw Mary blush and Linda twinkle maliciously.

"Darling Algy, you are *the* scandal of the moment. Did you know? Half everybody is saying you've sold all Monty's secrets to the Bolshevists, and that you're going to be shot at dawn in the Tower — and, darling, if you are, you *will* see about my having a front seat, won't you? Because what's the good of being a relation if it doesn't give you a pull?"

Algy laughed.

"I'll make a point of it. What are the other half saying?"

"That you're as *pure* as the driven snow," said Linda. "Algy, *darling*, do, do please tell us all about it. And if you did sell them, do tell me how, and where, and what you got for them, because I might try and collect something myself — I'm most awfully hard up. If I got Monty in the melting mood, I *might* get something out of him."

"Not you," said Giles — "he hates you like sin."

"Does he hate sin?" said the dark young man.

Algy said, "Apparently." He owed Linda something, and was always ready to pay.

"Yes, isn't it a shame?" she said. "And all because someone told him I said that it gave me the jitters to think of ever having another horse's neck — after meeting Maud, you know. And I adored them before, and someone told Monty, and he's been dead cuts with me ever since. Not *my* fault that Maud is the dead spit and image of a mare in the knacker's yard — now is it? But, Algy my angel, you haven't confided in us. Did you sell Monty, or didn't you? And what did you get for it? And are they going to shoot you at dawn?"

"The sentence has been commuted to an evening with you, my dear. Death by tongue-pricks — a nasty lingering affair. Be kind and get it over. Perhaps Giles will tell me what I am supposed to have done."

Fatal for Giles to hesitate, but he did — almost but not quite imperceptibly. Then he came in with a gay,

"You would be the last to hear about it. It's the most marvellous tale — all the Cabinet secrets gone down the drain, and your's the hand that loosed the plug."

There was no hesitation about Algy's laughter. If you didn't laugh at a thing like this, if you couldn't laugh at it, then you would go down under it and be dead, and damned, and done for. But Algy had no intention of being done for. He threw back his head and laughed, and it took him all he knew, but quite suddenly in the middle of it there came a strange rushing conviction that he was going to come out on top. He linked his arm with Mary Craster's and said,

"Marvellous! Poor Monty — has anyone broken it to him?"

Linda hung affectionately on his other arm.

"Darling, will he have to come and see you shot? In the front row. With Maud. He'll simply hate it — won't he? So humanitarian. But I suppose he'll have to. Home Secretaries do, don't they?"

"Too much imagination, my dear," said Algy. "Go and write a dime novel."

Linda shook her head.

"No, I'm going to do an anonymous autobiography. You know, *Malice in Mayfair*, or *Velvet and Venom*, or —"

"*Lispings of a Liar*," said Giles rudely.

"Jealous!" said Linda. "He won't be jealous about *me*, but he'd hate me to write a book — wouldn't you, darling?"

69

"Well, I'd have to settle up for the libel actions. And if you don't stop making love to Algy I shall probably break his head. Woman, your guests arrive. Behave!"

"It'll be Sylvia Colesborough," said Linda.

The front door of the flat opened and shut again. The maid announced, "Lady Colesborough and Mr Rooster."

Sylvia came in without hurry. She wore a pale gold frock. She had a radiance. The lights shone on her. Cyril Brewster, thin, dark, and earnest, followed her into the room. Linda surveyed him with surprise.

"Oh, Linda darling!" Sylvia kissed her. "I do hope you don't mind, but Francis couldn't come. He got a telephone call — from Birmingham, I think — they're generally from Birmingham — and he had to rush off. I do think being in business is a bore. But, darling, I'm afraid I've made rather a muddle, because I'd written you down for tomorrow, so I was going to dine with Mr Brewster, but when Francis said he couldn't come I remembered — you know how one does all of a sudden — so I thought if I brought him along it wouldn't put your table out."

Mr Brewster looked decidedly unhappy. The soul of correctness, he was being placed in a position which was irregular if not actually incorrect. The lady's husband had been asked. He was not the lady's husband. Far from it. He had only met her three times, and she had really given him no choice, she had simply brought him. Instead of her husband. And now it appeared that her husband hadn't been asked either. Lady Colesborough had always known he was going to be away.

"You said so all along, Sylvia — you know you did," said Linda, with an edge on her voice. Because really Sylvia was the limit, and the table could just be got to hold eight, but definitely wouldn't take nine. Well, it had got to — that was all. And anyhow it would make a frightfully good story, Sylvia trailing in about twenty minutes late with that awful stick Cyril and apologizing for Francis who hadn't been asked. She pushed aside Cyril's painstaking politeness with a laugh.

"The more the merrier, and if there isn't enough to go round, it shall be Giles. Or he and Algy can take it by turns. There's going to be too much of both of them if they don't watch it."

Amid indignant protests the door opened. Food began to come in, and they sorted themselves. The table stretched, as tables do, and there was plenty to eat, as there always was in Linda's house. She adored food, and could have lived on cream and potatoes without ever putting on a quarter of an ounce. Gay, racketing talk went to and fro. The red-haired girl, whose name was Muriel, told them she had been staying in a nudist colony and had felt an urge towards crinolines and large Victorian shawls ever since. She was wearing a shawl now, bright green and Spanish, and her very full black taffeta skirts swept the floor. Giles' friend with the superiority complex looked moody and said nothing. His name was Cedric, and his infatuation for lively red-haired Muriel had reached a point of which it was a fiery torment to himself and a source of extreme boredom to everyone else. Muriel's reactions those of the eternal feminine — a desire to prod, to poke, to stir the fire, and drop fresh fuel on the flame. Giles was hating her, and Linda despising him. The talk leapt flashing to and fro from pointed tongues.

Nobody said anything more about Algy. He was grateful, but he wondered why, discerning ultimately a queer substratum of loyalty that closed the ranks — and the tongues — against the outsider. Because Brewster — well there he was, just Brewster, Monty's Industrious Apprentice, not quite one of themselves. Algy would be thrown only to his own wolf pack to rend. And who said dog didn't eat dog? Wait and see.

CHAPTER
TEN

Masses of people came in after dinner. They played darts, and shove-halfpenny, and the ancient, never-dying games of Love and Scandal in their most up-to-date forms — fewer words to the game, but the same call of the eye, the same lift of the eyebrow that beckoned a man or killed a reputation in Egypt, Greece or Rome two thousand years ago.

Sylvia couldn't throw a dart straight to save her life. She regarded shove-halfpenny with horror. Why handle coppers if you hadn't got to? She didn't play the other games either. Algy took her to the window, lifted a bright green curtain, and let it fall again behind them.

"Look out here. Wait a minute till you can see. It's worthwhile."

They looked down as from a cliff on the dark tops of trees, all dark, all blurred, all moving in a wind which made no sound. More trees. Black houses away on the other side of the square, with bright lines showing here and there where a blind fell short or a curtain did not meet and just one window high up, bright and bare, with a black shadow coming and going in the room behind. And the river away to the left. Lights on it, moving lights, and a dark, slow stream, and the line of houses beyond, like an escarpment, blank and sheer.

To look out like this at night was to be soothed, consoled, assured of things immeasurably old and permanent — London — the river — trees and clouds — houses where people kindled fires from the same flame of hope which burned for ever and did not burn away. Things went on. You were up against it, you sweated blood, you won perhaps. And the game went on. Meanwhile this moment was good. Seen, Sylvia delighted and satisfied the eye. Unseen, she had the gift of silence. She stood with her shoulder touching his and leaned a little upon the sill, but did not speak. The good moment was shared. At least that is how it seemed to Algy. He heard the faintest of faint sighs, and thought it a tribute to the night.

"It's pretty good, isn't it?" he said.

"All those trees — and the river — like the country —" But her voice was flat.

A most horrible suspicion entered Algy's mind.

"Don't you like the country?"

"Oh, no." Surprise enlived her tone. 'Oh, no, I hate it — don't you? Especially in the dark. Why, I lived in the country for years. It was dreadful. We hadn't even got a car, and I do hate walking. I think I'd like to go back into the room if you don't mind — I do rather hate the dark."

Algy held the curtain and saw her pass beyond it. The light caught her gold hair and her gold dress as she went. But he did not follow her. He had been going to ask her about the Wessex-Gardners' week-end party,

74

but there would be time for that. He dropped the curtain, and turned to the river again. The moment had not been shared after all, but it was still good.

From behind him, in a sudden fierce whisper, came the voice of Cedric Blake.

"Muriel, it's no use — I can't stand it — you'll have to!"

The whisper broke, and close by the curtain the red-haired girl laughed under her breath.

"You're driving me mad!"

"I? You're driving yourself." Her voice was cool and scornful.

The curtain swayed inwards. Algy thought there was a snatched embrace. He thought he ought to say that he was there. He thought he had better not. Muriel's voice came in a pricking undertone.

"If you do that again —"

"What will you do?"

She gave a sudden melting laugh.

"I really don't know. Come and throw a dart."

Algy heaved a sigh of relief. He was about to lift the curtain and emerge, when he heard his own name. Mary Carster said with tears in her voice,

"It's perfectly horrible. How can they? I love Algy."

"Bless you, my dear," said Algy to himself. The refrain of a pleasanter song than *Gilderoy* hummed itself in his mind:

"Kind, kind and gentle is she,
Kind is my Mary."

It was James who was with her, and the inarticulate James was moved to reply.

"So do I. Rotten! I say, darling, you can't cry here. Do hold up."

"I'm not crying."

They moved away.

Algy stood frowning behind the curtain. As bad as that, was it? He heard Sylvia say sweetly and wearily,

"Oh, Mr Brewster — how kind! I would love a chair. I don't think I like sitting on the floor very much. You see, I don't want to spoil my dress."

"It's a very beautiful dress," said the earnest voice of Cyril Brewster. "It is almost worthy, if I may say so, of its wearer."

Algy controlled an inward spasm. What a fatuous ass Brewster was. No, not fatuous — that wasn't the right word at all. Simple, earnest, Victorian, bromidic — these were all much better adjectives.

"That's very nice of you," said Sylvia with evident pleasure.

This was the moment for Algy to come out. He meant to. He was going to. But the temptation to hear more of Cyril in a complimentary mood was too much for him. With his hand on the curtain he dallied, and was rewarded.

"There is a very beautiful line in the *Idylls of the King*," pursued Mr Brewster — "an extremely beautiful line in which someone — a man I think — expresses himself to the effect that he that loves beauty should go beautifully. I am almost sure that it was a man, and that the lady's name was Enid, in which case it was from the poem entitled *Enid and Geraint*. I cannot be entirely certain that my memory is accurate, as it is a good many years since I opened my Tennyson."

"I have a dreadful memory too," said Sylvia comfortably.

Algy blessed her, and would have given a good deal to see Cyril's face. He ought to come out though, he ought to come out.

His hand went to the curtain and stayed there, because Sylvia was saying,

"Is there something wrong about Mr Somers? I thought he was so nice."

On any other night of any other month Algy would have taken that cue, bowed with hand on heart, and most convincingly have guaranteed his niceness. But not tonight, not with this damnable thing hanging over him. He stayed where he was, and heard Brewster, politely embarrassed.

"Oh, there's nothing, Lady Colesborough — nothing at all. I really don't know who could have given you such an impression."

"Linda," said Sylvia — "Mrs Westgate, you know. I said how much I liked him and I thought I'd ask him to go to the Kensingtons' dance next week, and she said better not, and Francis wouldn't like it, but she wouldn't say why — and I did like him so much."

"Oh, but I assure you —"

Algy began to edge away towards the second window. He lost Cyril's embarrassed defence, but he managed to emerge from behind the end curtain without being noticed.

Sylvia sat lightly on one of the chromium-plated chairs in her golden dress. Mr Brewster occupied a jade-green cushion at her feet. Neither the colour nor the attitude became him. Darts were flying, a thought dangerously. There was a constant babel and babble of voices.

Algy found James Craster.

"Here," he said, "I want to know how serious is this damned story — for me, I mean?"

James was large, and fair, and taciturn. He took thought, and produced reluctant words.

"Damned serious, I'm afraid."

"People are believing it?"

"Not Mary and me."

"Thanks. Other people though?"

James took thought again, again found words — more words than usual.

"Perhaps not today. All saying can't believe such a thing."

"Depends how that's said." Algy's tone was grim.

James nodded, and saved a word.

"Tomorrow they'll be spreading it. Saying, 'Suppose he did.' Next day it'll be, 'Well, I always thought.' That's how it goes. Unless it's stopped. Better stop it quick. Get Lushington to stop it. That's my advice. Lies breed like flies."

Algy was rather grey. James hit hard. Once you got him going he'd say what he thought. No beating about the bush. No tact. A good friend.

He passed on, talked to Mary for a little, and found her gentle commonplaces a balm. She never said anything that you could label as wise or witty. She looked with her friendly eyes, and her voice was like running water, clear, and cool, and sweet. Algy esteemed James a lucky fellow.

When he saw Mr Brewster rise not very gracefully from his cushion at Sylvia's feet, he crossed over, sped Cyril on his way and annexed the vacant place. Sylvia, vaguely embarrassed, seemed about to be gone. Algy smiled at her.

"Do stay and talk to me, Lady Colesborough. Has he been warning you against me? Do tell me."

Sylvia responded with a smile, a little nervously, and said,

"Oh, no."

"I'm not really dangerous, you know, and we got on beautifully the other night, didn't we? Now let's talk about the country. Why do you hate it?"

"We were so poor," said Sylvia with simplicity.

Algy liked her for that. He pursued his ordered way. A very good reason.

"But do you hate it when you're not poor? You were at Wellings last week, weren't you? Do you hate a place like that? It's lovely, isn't it?"

"I suppose so," said Sylvia doubtfully. "In summer it might be. I like lights in the streets, and plenty of shops, and people."

Algy laughed. She looked like the sun and the moon and the stars, but she didn't like those things. She liked people and shops. He said,

"I expect there were plenty of people at Wellings, weren't there?"

"Well, it wasn't a big party."

"Who did you have?"

"Well, Poppy and Buffo — but of course it's their house. You know them, don't you?"

"Just a little."

"She has the most divine clothes." Sylvia's eyes waked into starry beauty. "She designs them herself, you know, and I can't think how she does it. I do think clever people are marvellous — don't you?"

"They're a menace," said Algy. "I always avoid them. Who else did you have?"

"Well, his brother — Buffo's brother Binks — and his wife, Constance. She isn't a bit like Poppy."

"And you and your husband?"

"Yes, but Francis was late for dinner because he couldn't get away — business is so tiresome that way — so I had to go down alone."

"The Lushingtons were there, weren't they?"

Sylvia nodded.

"They had just arrived when I got there, but we had to go off and dress for dinner almost at once."

She was quite pleased to prattle. With a very little trouble Algy discovered the geography of the house and the whereabouts of the guests. There was an east wing and a west wing. Buffo and Poppy were in the west wing, and so were Binks and Constance. The Lushingtons had the big suite at the end of the east wing, and the Colesboroughs were next to them — "And we each had a room and a bathroom. You know, it's dreadful how few bathrooms we've got at Cole

Lester — only three besides our own two, and I can't get Francis to see that it isn't enough."

They talked earnestly about bathrooms, and presently Algy got her back to Wellings again. It was possible to get her back, but not possible to keep her there. She broke away in the middle of a sentence and said,

"You're a friend of Gay's, aren't you?"

Algy said, "Yes," and wondered if it was true. He was Gay's friend last night, but last night was a long time ago. They stood together in the dark with anger flashing between them — hot anger — hot, dangerous anger. And someone had put Monty's envelope in his pocket, and Monty was being pressed to look no farther than his own household for the thief. Last night was a long way off. He wondered whether he was Gay's friend today, and he said,

"Oh, yes."

Sylvia went on babbling about Gay.

CHAPTER
ELEVEN

Gay waked with a start to realize that the telephone bell was ringing. She said something short and sharp, sat up, and switched on the light. Her watch made it half past twelve, an hour which seems quite early when you are out but feels like the middle of the night when you have gone to bed. It felt like the middle of the night to Gay. Who in this world and all could be ringing up at such a ghastly time? She sat listening and hoping against hope that the thing hadn't rung, or that, having rung without getting an answer, it wouldn't ring again.

It rang again — a very persevering effort.

Gay ran barefoot down the stairs, switching on lights as she went, a dressing-gown hung dolman-fashion across her shoulders and clutched together in front. Aunt Agatha would sleep through a duet between Big Ben and the Westminster Chimes. The staff firmly disregarded any telephone call between eleven at night and seven in the morning.

The bell was still ringing when Gay snatched the receiver and said in an abusive whisper,

"Who are you?"

But of course she might have guessed. Sylvia said in a plaintive voice,

"Oh, darling, you do sound cross."

"Homicidal!" said Gay. "What's the matter? Do you know what time it is?"

"Darling, it's quite early."

"That's because you're turning night into day. I was in bed and asleep, and I haven't even got my dressing-gown on properly. I've come down five flights of stairs, and the temperature is somewhere round about zero."

She heard Sylvia catch her breath.

"Darling, how did you hear it up five flights of stairs?"

This was pressure upon a wound. Gay spoke with bitterness.

"I didn't — no one could. That's why Aunt Agatha had a bell fixed up on my floor. It's supposed to be for the staff, but they just won't. Is this a talk on telephones, or do you really want anything?"

"Oh, I do." Sylvia's voice changed. "Gay, I'm so frightened — I just had to ring you up."

"What are you frightened of? What have you been doing?"

"Nothing — I haven't really. But I shall have to. It's — it's so dreadful to have it coming nearer and nearer."

"What are you talking about?"

"You see, I've been out all day. I went shopping with Poppy, and we lunched together, and then we watched a mannequin show, and I had three cocktail parties, and I was going to dine with Mr Brewster but fortunately I remembered about being engaged to Linda, and Francis had gone off to Birmingham or somewhere, so I took Mr Brewster instead. And I liked it awfully. I wore my gold dress, you know, and I had a lot of compliments —"

"Sylly, what are you talking about?"

"Linda Westgate's party. Oh, and your Algy Somers was there."

Gay denied him with vehemence.

"He's *not* my Algy Somers!"

"Oh, I thought he was." Sylvia was vague and amiable. "But perhaps you'd better not, because Linda and Francis wouldn't like it if I let him take me out. No, *really* — she meant there was something wrong, only she wouldn't tell me what it was, and Mr Brewster wouldn't either."

"Sylly, this is pure drivel. Have you got anything to say or haven't you? Because if you have, get on with it, and if you haven't, I'm going back to bed. There isn't any central heating in this house, and I've probably got frost-bite already."

Sylvia, in a temperature mounting to 70°, was without sympathy.

"You see," she pursued, "I quite forgot about it all day — at least not quite but almost — but as soon as I came in and got up to my own room I felt dreadful again, because I know he'll make me do it, and I simply can't think what will happen if Francis finds out. And he will — I'm sure he will. He — he guesses things, and comes down on you like lightning."

"Sylly, listen!" Gay spoke firmly. "You're not to do anything at all. If this man wants you to take papers for him, you're not to do it."

84

"I shall have to — he'll tell Francis if I don't."

"Tell Francis yourself, then you'll be all clear. If you take these papers you'll be in the worst hole you've ever been in in your life."

"Darling, it's not papers."

Gay stamped, and wished she hadn't. Her foot was cold, and the floor pure ice.

"You said it was."

"No, it's his keys — Francis' keys." Her tone suddenly brightened. "How stupid of me! I needn't have worried. Because Francis is away. He got a telegram and he went off, and of course he took his keys, so no one, not even that horrid Zero man, could make me do anything about them tonight. I can just go off to bed and not bother. And I needn't have rung you up, but I've loved talking to you. Good-night, darling."

Gay didn't say good-night. She pitched the receiver back on to its hook and ran violently up five flights of stairs to her room, where she took a flying leap into the bed and called her hot water bottle to witness that the telephone might ring itself blue in the face if it liked, but if it thought she was going to answer, it could think again.

Sylvia hung up at her end with a little satisfied sigh. It was beautifully simple. Francis wasn't here, and his keys weren't here, so she couldn't take them. Even Mr Zero must see that. She needn't have worried at all. She began to hum a little tune to herself as she moved to and fro in her room.

And then all of a sudden it came to her that Mr Zero would be waiting outside the dining-room window from one to two, and it would look so very odd if anyone saw him. They might think all sorts of things, or they might arrest him, and if he was arrested, there was no knowing what he might tell the police. She thought she had better go down and tell him to go away. She could open just a little bit of the dining-room window and say, "It's no good — Francis isn't here," and Mr Zero would go away and they could all go to bed. It was a very comfortable plan.

She looked at the little crystal clock beside her bed, and saw that it was a quarter to one. That would give her time to take off her gold dress and put it away and get into a dressing-gown. She could fill in the time with brushing her hair.

When she had done all these things, she looked at the clock again. Just on one o'clock. She opened her bedroom door and looked out. A light burned there all night. It was one of the things that made Sylvia feel safe and rich. Poor Mummy was always so dreadfully cross if you left a light on for a single minute. Of course she couldn't help it, poor darling — she just had to scrimp and save, but it was dreadfully wearing. So now a light burned all night long upon every floor, and Sylvia, waking and turning over, could see a golden thread lying across her door-sill and go to sleep again feeling oh, so thankful not to be poor Sylvia Thrale any more.

She went to the head of the stairs and looked over. She could see the drawing-room door, and the light shining on the pale green stair-carpet. That made her feel good too, because you couldn't expect a colour like that to wear, and it didn't matter — most joyfully it didn't matter.

She trailed her white crepe dressing-gown down to the next flight. From there she could see the hall, and a corner of the fireplace, and the dining-room door. Walls and woodwork were a pale, bright primrose. There was a scarlet rug, and a table, a screen and a clock in scarlet lacquer. As she came through the hall, the clock struck one with a keen, ringing note. She stood with her hand on the dining-room door and waited for the sound to die away. Then she went in, not putting on the light, but leaving the door wide behind her. She could find her way to the window in the dark, and what she had to say need not take a minute.

There were two windows of the old-fashioned sash type. She reached the nearer one and slid back the catch, standing between the heavy violet curtain and the glass. A coldness came from it. She shivered and pulled up the swansdown collar of her wrap. Then she stooped to raise the window.

It was heavy, but it moved. She heard it creak. Then she heard something else — a footstep just outside, crossing the pavement, coming quickly up to the door. She pressed her face to the glass. Suddenly, terribly, she was afraid. She couldn't really see anything. There was no lamp very near, and the porch run out over the steps with pillars upon either side. They cut off what light there was. She had only seen a shadow, but she heard a horrifying and familiar sound, the little rattle which a latchkey makes when it is put into the lock, and hard upon that the click of the latch. The door swung in, swung back. The inner door swung in. A cold air came with it into the hall — through the open dining-room door. Sylvia turned round, flattening herself behind the curtain, because it was Francis who had come into his own house in the middle of the night — it couldn't be anyone else but Francis.

And he would want to know what she was doing down here in her dressing-gown. Sylvia, whose stupidity had driven Gay to desperation, was not at all stupid about this. She ceased in fact to be Sylvia Colesborough at all. She was immemorial woman, and there, on the other side of the open door, was immemorial man, a creature to be deceived. If she had been capable of thought at all, she would have thought, "I must hide," and have remained cowering behind her curtain. But she did not think. She ran out into the middle of the dining-room and called in a plaintive voice,

"Oh, Francis, is that you? Do put on the light. I can't see where I am."

The light went on. Francis Colesborough stood by the door with his hand on the switch. At this moment he looked his age. He had fair hair with a sprinkle of grey in it, grey eyes, hard and intent, a certain elegance of bearing. His skin lacked colour. The light which he had turned on picked out the lines of fatigue about eyes and mouth. He said with a kind of angry impatience,

"What are you doing, Sylvia?"

She smiled that lovely vague smile of hers.

"I wanted a biscuit — I thought I could find them in the dark. And then I heard you and went to look out of the window."

His hand dropped rather heavily from the switch.

"You weren't expecting me?"

She had found the biscuits. She picked out two or three and turned with them in her hand.

"Did you say you were coming back?"

"No, I didn't."

She began to tell him about the Westgates' party.

"Are you glad to see me?" he said abruptly in the middle of a sentence.

Sylvia trailed towards him in her lovely white wrap, offered a cheek to be kissed, yawned a little and said,

"But I'm always pleased to see you, darling."

CHAPTER
TWELVE

"It was in my pocket," said Algy Somers.

Montagu Lushington looked at the creased envelope which had come out of Algy's tail-pocket the night before. He said nothing. Algy went on.

"It's that envelope — there isn't any doubt about it at all. I didn't read the address, as I told you. I didn't know that I had looked at the envelope, but as soon as I saw that blot I knew I had seen it before, and where. It's shiny where the ink has dried, and I suppose that must have caught my eye, and I remembered it afterwards, though I didn't notice it at the time."

Montagu Lushington looked up.

"The envelope that was taken out of my despatch-case."

"Yes, sir."

"The empty envelope." There was a little weight on the second word.

Algy's face was set and grave. He said, "Yes, sir" again.

"And planted on you — put into your tail-pocket —" The slow almost meditative tone quickened suddenly. "With what object?"

Algy's face did not change, or his voice. He said,

"I've thought about that. It would support the theory that the papers were taken before you went down to Wellings."

"If it had been found on you — yes."

"It was intended to be found. I found it too soon, that's all. Or perhaps I was meant to find it. It may have been part of an attempt to stampede me — I don't know. There's a lot of talk going on. I was at the Westgates' last night. All Linda's crowd had got the story."

Mr Lushington wished — profanely — that someone would tell him how people got hold of these things.

"Well, they do," said Algy. "The men tell their wives, and the women tell each other — everyone adds a little. But they all know that important papers have gone missing, and most of them are half way to believing I took them. Somewhere about day after tomorrow they'll be quite sure I did. Then it's finish for me."

Montagu Lushington looked down at the envelope again.

"I don't see why this was planted on you."

Algy had one of those flashes. He said,

"Has no one suggested having my rooms searched?"

He got a quick upward glance. There was a pause, and Lushington said,

"I should not have entertained such a suggestion."

"But it was made?" Algy's tone warmed a little.

"I think that is a question which should not be put."

"But I do put it, sir. I don't see how I'm to meet this thing unless I know what I'm up against."

"Very well then, you may take it that the suggestion has been made."

"By whom?" Algy was pale.

"Do you expect me to tell you that?" said Montagu Lushington.

"Yes, I do, sir. You have just asked me why this envelope should have been planted in my pocket. I say it was planted in order that it might be found there. How was it going to be found there? My rooms were to be searched. Don't you think I have a right to know who has been suggesting that my rooms should be searched?"

Montagu Lushington said abruptly, "It was Carstairs. That makes nonsense of your suggestion, but the person who planted the envelope might have had knowledge of the line which Carstairs was taking — there is that."

"I'm not making any suggestion about Mr Carstairs — he's out of the question. But someone thought, or hoped, that there would be a search, and was willing to take a risk in order to make sure that something would be found. If you had authorized the search, and that envelope had been found in my coat, no one in the world would have believed that I was innocent. It would have been absolutely damning."

Montagu Lushington said, "Yes." Then, after a pause, "When do you think it was planted, and how?"

"Well, I found it last night when I was dressing to go to the Westgates', and it wasn't there the day before. At least, it wasn't there till four o'clock, because Barker — that's the man at my rooms — had the suit to press and lay out. I've asked him, and he's quite sure that there was nothing in any of the pockets. He put the things out for me somewhere about four o'clock, and then he and his wife went out. They go over to see her mother, and if I'm dining out they don't hurry back. I meant to dine out, but Mr Carstairs gave me the Babington stuff to type, and when I saw I wasn't going to get done in time, I rang up and said I couldn't get round till after dinner — and I didn't get done till a quarter to nine. The point is that I had to rush back and dress in a hurry. If the envelope had been in my pocket then, I don't think I should have noticed it."

"You mean someone might have got into your rooms between four and nine and have planted it then?"

"Yes, sir."

Montagu Lushington looked at him keenly.

"Very anxious to prove that it wasn't so likely to have been done later, aren't you, Algy?"

The blood came up into Algy's face. He said,

"No, sir."

"Oh, not unnaturally. Now I think we'll have the rest of your evening."

Algy stiffened a little.

"I called for a girl, and we went to the Ducks and Drakes."

"Her name?"

"Gay Hardwicke."

Montagu frowned slightly.

"Hardwicke — there's a Miss Agatha Hardwicke who bombards me and the papers with letters on the subject of capital punishment. She's secretary of some society or other. Rather a terrifying female."

"An aunt," said Algy gloomily. "Gay is staying with her. They're cousins of Lady Colesborough's."

He got another keen look.

"Known this young lady long?"

"About three months, sir."

"Well, you took her to the Ducks and Drakes. Were you alone, or in a party?"

"We went there alone, but we joined up with the Wessex-Gardners."

"What!" It was more of an exclamation than a word. A disturbed look crossed Montagu Lushington's face. "I should like to know who you danced with."

"Poppy Wessex-Gardner, Sylvia Colesborough, and Gay — mostly with Gay."

"Could one of them have put the envelope in your pocket?"

"Not while we were dancing."

"But you sat out?"

"We sat at a table and had drinks, and things to eat — I hadn't had any dinner."

"Yes, it could have been done then. You agree?"

"I suppose so."

"Who were the men of the party?"

"Wessex-Gardner and his brother. His brother's wife was there too. And a man called Danvers — I don't know anything about him — and Brewster."

"I didn't know Brewster went to night-clubs."

Algy laughed, not very cheerfully.

"He doesn't. Mrs Wessex-Gardner dragged him, and he's fallen for Sylvia Colesborough — a hopeless, respectful passion — she didn't even know he was there half the time."

"I can imagine that! What was this man Danvers like?"

"A bit of an outsider, I thought — the I'll-tell-the-world-I-did-it touch. He seemed to go down very well with Mrs Wessex-Gardner."

"Yes," said Montagu Lushington — "an old friend. At least so I gathered."

"What — he was at Wellings?"

Lushington shook his head.

"Not quite. He was expected, but he didn't turn up — at least not on the crucial Saturday. I believe he came over on the Sunday afternoon, but Maud and I had motored over to Hindon, so we did not see him. I wish now that we had, because it comes to this — any one of these people could have put that envelope in your pocket."

Algy thought for a moment.

"I suppose they could —" he said.

CHAPTER
THIRTEEN

Algy had plenty to think about all day. Monty had been very decent. "Stick to your job, and stick to your ordinary way of life. Go about the show yourself. Behave as if the whole thing was too ridiculous to be answered. That's my advice to you both as a member of my family and as a member of my staff." It was good advice too, and it fell in with Algy's mood, which was a fighting one. All the same it was easier said than done. Carstairs, always remote, now hardly appeared to be aware of him at all. Communications reached him by way of Brewster, and Brewster, nervously correct, made things worse by a hint of embarrassment and a tinge of apology. Not a nice day at all.

The worst part was the recurrent remembrance of Gay looking at him with serious eyes and asking him what he would do if someone tried to blackmail him. He had been trying hard not to remember it, but it kept gate-crashing in among his thoughts, and behind it there came, sidling, peeping, whispering, a whole crowd of perfectly idiotic suspicions, fancies, fears. If Gay was being blackmailed, what was the threat, the compulsion? You can't blackmail a girl with just nothing at all.

You've got to have a hold over her. What sort of mess had Gay got herself into?

He revolted sharply. She wasn't that sort. He felt an anger which surprised and discomfited him. He felt also a burning desire to weigh in and knock the blackmailer's teeth through the back of his head.

He tried to remember what she had said. She had flared up. He had a vivid recollection of how she had looked with the bright angry colour in her cheeks. And she had said, "What do you think I've done?" and they had been very near a quarrel. And afterwards — afterwards she had said that what the blackmailer wanted wasn't money, but something dreadful. One of those gate-crashing thoughts got in a word here. With perfect succinctness it observed, "He might have wanted her to put that envelope in your pocket."

She could have done it, and she was the only one who could have done it. He had known that all along. She could have done it in the taxi. She could have done it at the Ducks and Drakes. And she could have done it without any risk . . . He had a good deal of difficulty in keeping his mind on his work.

When he went out to lunch an enterprising representative of the brighter press waylaid him.

"Mr Somers?"

Algy said, "Not particularly," and the young man looked pained.

"Now, Mr Somers, I'd like to have your story."

Algy gazed at him all solemnity.

"I don't use them."

A faint shade passed over the young man's face.

"Now, Mr Somers — what's the use? Everyone knows about the missing papers. You would naturally like to have the story presented from the right angle. Our circulation —"

"I prefer a hot water bottle," said Algy. He walked at a brisk pace, the young man beside him, notebook in hand, incessantly vocal. "For the exclusive rights . . . And it would be so very much to your advantage . . . I think you can hardly realize —"

Algy smiled upon him.

"Perhaps it's night starvation. Have you tried Horlick?"

"But, Mr Somers —"

"Walk the Barratt way," said Algy with bonhomie.

The encounter cheered him a good deal. He lunched, and rang Miss Gay Hardwicke up. The conversation did not take quite the line he had intended. He had meant to be polite and a little detached. Unfortunately it was not Gay who came to the telephone. The voice which said, "Who is there?" was the kind of voice that takes the chair at public meetings. He could picture it addressing a conference of head mistresses. It recalled painful interviews with an aunt who had been a strong believer in corporal punishment for the young.

He said, "Can I speak to Miss Gay Hardwicke?" and was rather proud of himself for having the courage.

The voice called, "Gay!" on a ringing note, and Gay arrived rather breathless from the stairs.

Algy was too much relieved to be aloof.

Gay said, "Oh, it's you?" And then, "That was Aunt Agatha. What is it?"

The sound of her voice did something to the gate-crashers. They cast sickly looks at one another, and got into corners. Algy said,

"Come out tonight, Gay — will you? I want to talk to you."

Gay said, "Well —" in a tone which she hoped would sound doubtful, and was rewarded.

"Please, Gay, I must see you — I must talk to you."

"I can't dine. Aunt Agatha's got some of her committee coming. She'll be peeved if I'm not in to dinner, but I don't think they'll want me afterwards."

"Same as last time?"

"Yes, that will do."

"All right, I'll be round at half past nine."

By half past nine Gay was more than ready to drag herself away from an earnest committee which had been talking about executions for an hour and a half.

"You've no idea how *grim*. I'm converted absolutely, but I simply couldn't have listened to them for another minute. I feel as if I'd gone pale green all over."

"The bits I can see are all right," said Algy, as the light of a street-lamp slid over them.

She came closer and slipped a hand through his arm.

"Where are we going? I want to have my mind distracted."

"Would you mind awfully if it was the Ducks and Drakes again?"

"No. Why?"

"I'll tell you later on."

But at first they danced. And then the star turn held the floor, an apparently boneless girl dressed in her own brown skin and some strings of beads which caught the light and flashed it back in ruby, emerald, and sapphire. She had a black fuzz of hair, eyes like pools of ink, and the largest, reddest mouth and the whitest teeth in the world. To the sound of strange percussion instruments and the rhythmic beat of a drum the brown girl twisted, writhed, and swayed. Her black eyes rolled, her white teeth gleamed. There was a fascinating play of muscle under the shining skin. She really didn't seem to have any bones at all.

When it was over Algy said, "Do you mind if we talk now?" and Gay said, "No," and then wondered if she had been a fool, and a fool to come out with him. She threw a quick look at him and found him serious, panicked a little, and said quickly,

"There's that Mr Danvers who was with the Wessex-Gardners the other night."

Algy was already aware of Mr Danvers. He had, in fact, come here in the hope of seeing Mr Danvers, who appeared to be an *habitué*. He said casually,

"Oh, yes, he's often here, I believe. Do you know him?"

"Not really. I met him here the other night."

"Did you dance with him?"

She made a little face.

"Once."

"And what did you think of him?"

"Oh, I hated him," said Gay cheerfully.

"Do you mind telling me why?"

"I'd love to tell you why. I've been wanting to let off steam ever since."

"Why, what did he do?"

"He didn't do anything. He looked over the top of my head and told me how he had made a steel combine toe the line."

Algy burst out laughing.

"My poor child! I'm afraid I can't break his head for that."

"No — it's a pity, isn't it? And when he had finished about the steel combine he began about a gas corporation — he's got a tame one that eats out of his hand. And he rolls in wealth, but he's very careful about girls — not to give them any encouragement, you know."

"Can you look me in the eye and swear he told you that?"

"No, darling. That was Poppy Wessex-Gardner. Being kind, you know, so that I shouldn't have any false hopes raised through being danced with and having heart-to-heart confidences about gas. And I said, 'Oh, no, Mrs Wessex-Gardner,' and, 'Oh, yes, Mrs Wessex-Gardner,' and looked meek, and my old black dress helped a lot, so she thawed a little and let me off with a caution instead of sending for the court executioner and saying, 'Off with her head!'"

"My child, you rave."

"I know I do. It's Aunt Agatha's capital punishment people." Her voice changed suddenly. "Why do you want to know about Mr Danvers, and what do you want to know about Mr Danvers?"

Algy leaned nearer and said in a low, direct voice,

"I want to know whether he's your blackmailer, Gay."

They were at a table in an alcove. There was no one near enough to hear, but anyone might have seen Gay's change of colour and her startled look. She said all in a hurry,

"Why should he be?" And then, "I haven't got a blackmailer! Don't call him mine!" After which she took breath and said in a serious voice, "Algy, what on earth do you mean?"

Algy did not answer at once. He took time to look at Gay, time to be sure that he trusted her, time to tell himself that he had been a fool. He said at last,

"When we were here the other night something was slipped into one of my pockets, and I'm wondering who did it. You asked me what I would do if someone tried to blackmail me, and then you were angry because I thought you meant that someone was blackmailing you. I wish you'd tell me the rest."

"There isn't any more, and if there was, I couldn't tell you. What did you find in your pocket — a love letter?"

"Something that had been stolen."

"Algy — not really! How thrilling!"

Algy said, "No," And then after a pause, "Damnable."

Her face changed.

"Algy, *please*. What is it? Do tell me."

He shook his head.

"I can't. You'll probably hear about it — there's a considerable amount of chat going on. But I'd rather you didn't say anything about the envelope being put into my pocket."

Her eyes opened so widely that the lights shone down into them as the sun shines into dark peaty water, lightening its colour, filling it with floating golden specks. He thought with a faint shock of surprise, "Her eyes aren't dark at all, they're amber. It's the shade of the lashes that makes them look black."

She caught her breath and opened her lips to speak, but didn't speak. She was remembering something, and trying not to remember it.

Algy said quickly, "What is it, Gay?" and she said nothing. And then,

"Why should anyone put an envelope in your pocket?"

Algy leaned an elbow on the table.

"I think someone had the kind thought that my rooms might be searched, and that it might be found there. Fortunately I found it myself."

Gay leaned over the table too.

"Algy — how horrid! Who could possibly —"

"That's what I'm going to find out."

She spoke quickly.

"You're not — in any trouble? It's not — it's not serious?"

"It might be."

"How?" The word was rather breathless.

He looked away from her because it was dangerous to be so near, to see her eyes so soft and anxious — for him. He said in a studiously quiet voice,

"Someone's trying to get me into trouble. If they bring it off, I should be finished as far as my present job is concerned, and as far as politics are concerned. There'd be a black mark against me. But they're not going to bring it off. I'm going to get to the bottom of it and clear myself."

"You can't tell me about it?"

He did look at her then. This was a Gay he had not seen before — serious, troubled. He said,

"I don't think so. You'll hear the talk — you're bound to."

Her lip quivered. She put up her hand to it like a child and shook her head.

"I wouldn't listen — you know that. Won't you tell me?"

"I don't think I must, Gay."

She looked away with a quick turn of the head as if he had hurt her. He found his hand on her arm.

"Gay — don't. I'd like to tell you, but it's not my affair."

Gay jumped up.

"Come and dance! That's what we came here for, isn't it? Oh, no — you did say something about wanting to talk to me — didn't you? But of course — how stupid of me — you only meant to find out whether someone had been blackmailing me into putting stolen whatnots into your pocket."

"Gay!" He had got up too. There was the width of the table between them, and hard breaking waves of anger.

Gay's head was high and her eyes bright.

"Well, that was it, wasn't it! *Wasn't* it? You can't say it wasn't — can you?"

Algy was quite as angry as she was — angrier perhaps, because he had the disadvantage of a guilty conscience. He smiled and said,

"Is this an invitation to the waltz?"

Gay considered. Even in the middle of her just indignation she could be practical. If you quarrel with your young man at a night-club, proper pride demands that you either go off with someone else or that you take a taxi home. As the only possible alternative to Algy was Mr Danvers, and going home would mean more capital punishment, she blenched. Her lip twitched and she broke into an angry laugh.

"For tuppence I'd catch the Danvers' eye!"

Algy produced the tuppence and held it out.

"This will be number two in our programme entitled 'Why Girls Take Gas.' Go on — I dare you!"

"Algy, you're a beast!"

He put the coppers in his pocket, slipped his arm round her waist, and said,

"Fierce — aren't you? Come along and dance."

CHAPTER
FOURTEEN

They had made their way as part of a rhythmically moving crowd to the other side of the room, when Gay looked across the packed floor and said in a surprised voice,

"There's Sylvia — and Francis."

Algy looked with admiration at Sylvia in white, and with interest at the big fair man beside her.

"They're a good-looking couple."

"Yes. I only met him once — and at the wedding, you know. I was a bridesmaid. But you couldn't miss him, could you?"

The Colesboroughs penetrated the dancing mass and were absorbed, but the two fair heads could be distinguished. Algy followed them with his eyes, then turned to Gay.

"My word, she's lovely! What's she really like, Gay?"

Gay lifted eyes with a sparkle in them.

"You've danced with her, darling."

"You always call me darling when you're annoyed. Does one know what a person is really like after dancing with her once?"

Gay said, "You very often think you do when it's someone like Sylvia."

He let that go, and said in a serious voice,

"I really want to know. Tell me what she's like."

Gay dropped her lashes. She said,

"I've known her all my life. I've never seen her lose her temper."

"Yes?" said Algy in an encouraging tone. "She looks like that. What else?"

"She likes beautiful things."

"That's not a crime."

The lashes went up again.

"I didn't say it was."

"Did you mean that she likes herself?"

Gay's eyes sparkled suddenly.

"Darling, how prig! That's not a crime either. I love myself very, very much, and so do you."

"Yes — I think I do," said Algy in an odd voice.

Gay's cheeks burned.

"I love my self, and you love your self," she said as quickly as her tongue would go.

"I didn't mean that," said Algy. "You know what I meant, but I oughtn't to have said it, so I'm not going to say it again, but when this mess is cleared up —"

"We were talking about Sylvia," said Gay in a hurry.

"Yes — go on telling me about her."

"There isn't anything more to tell."

"You mean that?"

Gay said, "Yes."

"Nothing behind all that except a sweet temper?"

"The house is practically unfurnished," said Gay.

The music stopped. As they went towards their table, the Colesboroughs emerged from a group that was breaking up. The Westgates were in the centre of it with Sir James Harringay, the well-known K.C. Linda waved a hand. Giles nodded. Sir James looked, and looked away. It was not quite a cut, but it was as near as makes no difference. Gay saw what was impossible to miss — she saw Algy's jaw stiffen. She rushed into a "How do you do?" to Francis Colesborough, and then tingled lest she should have done the wrong thing. But Francis made himself pleasant, asked why he hadn't seen her since the wedding, said she must come down to Cole Lester, and was polite to Algy. Sylvia put her hand through Gay's arm and pinched it — an old signal that meant, "I want to speak to you." They passed on.

When they were at their table, Algy said, "What about Colesborough? He's not an uninhabited house, I take it."

Gay said, "No" in a doubtful voice. "I don't know him — I think he's good to Sylvia — I think she's afraid of him — I don't know him.

They danced again. When the final chord blared out Sylvia came to them through the crowd. Algy could not help saying, "How beautifully she moves." There was no hurry, no effort. The crowd did not seem to impede her. She took her own easy, floating way. But there was no ease in the look that met Gay's and spoke an urgent message. It said, "I must see you," but her words were commonplace enough.

"Darling, I'm coming to bits. Be an angel and pin me."

She carried Gay off. In the cloakroom, at the farthest glass, she began in a rapid whisper.

"I simply had to see you. It's too dreadful. I don't know what to do."

The cloakroom was empty except for a stolid sandy-haired attendant who seemed more than half asleep. Gay said in a exasperated undertone,

"What on earth has happened now?"

Sylvia clutched her.

"Nothing — not yet — but it will. I mean, he'll make me do it — and I'm so frightened."

"Sylly, we can't stay here. If you want to say anything, say it."

"I *am*," said Sylvia with tears in her eyes. "You know when I rang you up last night, and I thought it was going to be all right because Francis was away so of course there wasn't anything I could do about his keys, and I was quite happy, but then it came over me that that Zero man would be waiting on the doorstep, and I thought how odd it would look — if anyone saw him, you know — so I thought I'd just go down and tell him it wasn't any good, and just as I was getting the window open —"

"Why the window?"

"The dining-room window," said Sylvia, as if that explained everything. "I was behind the curtain, and, darling, I nearly died, because just as I was getting it to move I heard his latchkey, and there he was in the hall."

"Who was?"

"Francis, darling — I told you I heard his latchkey. And of course he wanted to know what I was doing downstairs in my dressing-gown, and just as I got him soothed he saw the curtain move, and when he found

I'd been opening the window he was quite dreadful —
all suspicious, like a person in a play. As if I *would!*"

Sylvia's moral indignation was most edifyingly genuine.
She would steal — and call it something else — but to
her last breath she would remain an honest woman.

Gay released herself. She wanted to be firm and
impressive, and it is difficult to impress when you are
being clutched. She said,

"Sylvia, if you don't tell Francis, something dreadful
will happen."

Sylvia opened lovely startled eyes.

"There *couldn't* be anything worse. You don't know
him. And you're not letting me tell you what happened.
We had a dreadful night, and in the morning, just as I
dropped off to sleep, that horrible Zero man rang up
again."

"Where was Francis?"

"Having his bath. He always gets up most frightfully
early, and I thought I *was* going to get a little sleep."

Gay was definitely unsympathetic.

"That doesn't matter. What did the creature want?"

"Those papers," said Sylvia in a frightened whisper
— "a packet of letters tied up with a rubber band. He
says they're in Francis' safe and he's simply got to have
them. He says they belong to him. He says I'll know
which they are because they've got Zero on them. He
says it's too late to get the keys for him now — he says
I must get the papers myself."

Gay cast an anxious look at the attendant, but the
sandy lashes lay on the pasty cheeks, the hands were
folded in an ample lap, and a sound which came very

near to being a snore reassured her. She turned back to Sylvia.

"Sylly, you can't!" she said.

"I must — he says so. If I don't he'll tell Francis, and I'd rather be dead. And we're going down to Cole Lester tomorrow — because of the window being opened, you know. And I'm to take the letters down and give them to him — in the yew walk, like when I met him before."

"What time?" said Gay.

Sylvia caught her breath. "He's very frightening," she said. "He knows everything. He knows when I go to bed, and he knows Francis sits up writing in his study till half past one. So that's when I'm to take the papers. The servants will be in bed, and Francis will be in his study, and everyone will think I'm asleep. And I'm to go to the alley, and he'll be outside to take them through the window in the hedge. And if Francis finds out, I think he'll kill me."

Gay felt a sudden horror between them. She caught her breath and said quickly,

"Don't talk nonsense, Sylly!"

"It isn't nonsense," said Sylvia Colesborough. Her eyes widened. A shiver went over her. The lovely natural tints faded from her face. She looked past Gay as if she saw something behind her in the empty room and said in a half whisper, "I'm frightened — I *am* frightened, Gay."

Gay said, "Tell Francis. you mustn't do what this man wants you to. If you tell Francis you'll be safe, because he won't have a hold over you any more."

Sylvia choked down a sob.

"I can't — I can't — you don't understand — and you don't know Francis — I can't tell him."

Gay said, "Let me," and saw Sylvia's face go grey.

She caught at Gay and stood there trying to speak. The words wouldn't come, not till Gay got her into a chair and knelt beside her saying every soothing thing that she could think of. Then the words came with a flood of tears.

"You mustn't — you won't — you *can't!* Oh, Gay!"

Gay was ready to promise her the moon. The attendant still snored, but she would be bound to wake if Sylvia went on crying like this. In any case what could she do except say, and swear, and mean it, that of course she wouldn't dream of telling Francis what Sylvia had told her in confidence?

This had the desired effect, and with no more than a tear or two entangled in those long lashes, Sylvia gazed at her reproachfully.

"Darling, you did upset me. I've always told you things, and I never dreamed you would think of telling anyone, *especially* Francis."

Gay was relieved but provoked.

"Well, I never meant to," she said.

Sylvia turned to the mirror.

"You've made me look *too* frightful." She produced cream and powder from a be-diamonded bag and began to repair the damage. "You know, Gay, you really ought to be careful not to upset people. I might have *fainted*, and then what would you have done?"

Gay couldn't help laughing.

112

"Rubbish, Sylly — you've never fainted in your life!"

Sylvia looked back over her shoulder quickly, as if there might be something behind her.

"I thought — I was going to — I felt —" She shivered again, then went back to rubbing cream into her face. "I don't generally put any colour on, but I think I'd better have a little — don't you?"

Gay said, "Yes, I think so."

"But I'm sure it will be all right really. I mean, if I do what this Zero man wants me to this time, he won't ever ask me anything again — he's absolutely promised that. You see, he says the letters are really his and Francis won't let him have them. And of course, he says, he could go to law and get them that way, but it would cost such a lot that we might all be ruined, so it's much better for me to do what he wants, and I've told him it's no good his thinking I'll do anything more, because I won't. I really feel quite all right about it now."

She got up, smiled at her own reflection, slipped her arm into Gay's and said,

"I don't know what made me feel like that. It was horrid — just as if something dreadful was going to happen."

CHAPTER
FIFTEEN

It was next day that it began to dawn upon Algy that Brewster was sorry for him. The remoteness of Carstairs continued. The atmosphere of the office was glacial in the extreme. Brewster, in the capacity of intermediary, wore a worried and deprecating air. Impossible as the day wore on to escape the conviction that Brewster was being kind. Algy, conscious of ingratitude, wished that Brewster wouldn't. In the role of Samaritan he found him frankly intolerable. He preferred him as a human encyclopaedia. This being Saturday, there was, however, only half a day to be endured. There was hope that the kindness of Brewster might have expended itself before they met again on Monday morning. Possibly, though not probably, Carstairs might have thawed. Anyhow, whatever had happened or was going to happen, Algy intended to play golf. Too much office — too many stuffy rooms — too many feelings, thoughts, suspicions. He had a conviction that fresh air and exercise were most urgently required.

The new Bentley had never run better. He returned to town a good deal soothed. He had played like an angel, done a 76 off the back tees, and taken half a sovereign off Smithers, who was as sick as mud.

He came whistling up the stairs, and was arrested half way by Barker, who emerged soundlessly from the dining-room and informed him that a lady had been ringing him up — "No name, sir, and no message, except that she said she would be ringing again later."

Algy went on up to his room and proceeded to have a bath. The capacity to produce boiling hot water at any hour of the day or night was one of Mrs Barker's shining virtues. She had others. Her pastry was a dissolving dream, her pancakes melted in the mouth, and her soups were of an infinite variety. With these things she had doubtless ensnared the heart, head and stomach of Barker, who had rightly esteemed them above the attractions of face and figure. Vast and shapeless was Mrs Barker, small of eye and scanty of hair, emerging only at the rarest intervals from the underground kitchen where she stoked fires and meditated rare sauces and omelettes.

Algy wallowed in his bath and anticipated his dinner with pleasure. When the telephone bell rang he cursed it bitterly. Never is a hot bath so agreeable as when you have to leave it. Never is the voice of a friend less welcome than when you listen to it girt with a hastily snatched towel. Algy dripped, Algy cursed, Algy contorted his agreeable features into a scowl. He said, "Who's there?" in the voice that means, "Why weren't you drowned at birth?" and heard Gay Hardwicke say rather breathlessly,

"Oh, Algy, is that you?"

It was the sort of ridiculous thing that girls did say. Because if it was, why ask him, and if it wasn't, why call him Algy? But the scowl subsided into a mere frown as he replied,

"It's me. I'm dripping all over the Barkers' new carpet."

"Why?" said Gay in an interested voice.

"Because I was in the middle of having a bath."

He distinctly heard her laugh. Then she said,

"Darling, how grim! Go away and finish having it and then come back all clean and tidy and ring me up."

"Can't you tell me what you want?"

She laughed again, a little nervously he thought.

"Not whilst you drip. I want you in your very best mood. You sounded perfectly ferocious when you asked who I was." She hung up, and Algy went back to his bath.

When he rang up ten minutes later she enquired anxiously after his temper.

"I thought it sounded quite feverish just now."

"It's in the pink," said Algy.

"Really? Because I want to ask you something, and I'd rather know beforehand if you're likely to blow up."

Algy smiled at the pattern of humming-birds and roses on his sitting-room wall.

"No explosives on the premises. You wrong me, my child. I am known as Algernon, the man who never lost his temper."

"How awful that sounds! Has anyone really ever called you Algernon?"

"My grandmother did. I can just remember her saying, 'Here are threepence, Algernon. Do not spend them all at once.'"

"And did you?"

"Of course. And then she died and left me a great deal more than threepence, bless her. Did I ring you up to talk about grandmothers? I mean, was that the original intention, or were you just asking after my temper?"

Gay's voice dropped. She said,

"Well, I want to ask you something."

Algy took her up.

"Last time you said that, I offered you half my kingdom, but you only wanted to talk about being blackmailed. What is it this time?"

"Cars," said Gay in a burst of confidence. "I mean your car. I mean —"

"What do you mean? You're not getting anywhere, you know."

"Well, that's just what I want to do. I want to get somewhere, and — I don't see how I can without a car, and — I wondered — whether you'd lend me yours —"

Algy stopped smiling. He stared at the nearest humming-bird and received the impression that it was rather a sinister fowl. He said quite slowly,

"You want me to lend you my car. When?"

"Tonight," said Gay.

"Can you drive? Have you got a licence?"

"I've got a licence. I've had lessons."

Algy burst out laughing.

"My child, if bent on suicide, why involve my Bentley?"

A very small voice came back to him.

"I don't know. I thought perhaps — you would —"

Algy was smitten. She sounded like a forlorn child. He said,

"My dear, don't be idiotic. If you want to go anywhere, I'll drive you — you know that."

He could feel her hesitation. Odd to feel it like that along the wire. And then her voice:

"I don't — know. Algy, would you — would you really?"

"Of course I would. I will."

He heard her catch her breath.

"And not ask questions, or want to know where I'm going and what it's all about?"

"I'm afraid I'll have to know where you're going or I can't get you there. Gay, what's this all about? Can't you tell me?"

"No — no, I can't — I'll have to find some other way."

"What time do you want to be fetched?"

"I think about ten. It'll take about two hours. I want to be there by twelve."

An almost inaudible whistle escaped from Algy.

"Is this an all-night show?"

"Oh, I don't think so. I think we ought to be back by three."

"Gay!"

She found words suddenly.

"Algy, I don't know why you should. There isn't any reason really. But I've got to, and it would make all the difference to know you were there — standing by. Only I can't tell you anything, and if you're going to ask questions —"

"I won't," said Algy.

"Because I could go alone."

"You're not going alone. I'm calling for you at ten," said Algy, and hung up.

CHAPTER
SIXTEEN

The Bentley ran smoothly between dark hedgerows. London was a long way behind them. Everyone in the world was a long way off. They moved in their own light, a full, clear beam stretching out before them, stretching on. They had talked whilst the streets were about them, but now they were silent. The talk had moved lightly on the surface and never broken it.

When Algy asked, "Where do you want to go?" Gay had a map to show him, ready folded.

"The name of the place is Colebrook. It's about thirty-five miles."

"Then it won't take anything like two hours."

And then it was, "When did you learn to drive?"

"Last summer when we were at Cromer, darling."

"And you passed your test?"

"You're very interested."

Algy said, "Yes. You haven't told me if you passed. Did you?"

There was pause. Then Gay said hotly,

"He was a perfect beast! How was I to know that the thing was going to do a sort of wiggle and run into a pillar-box?"

"My poor child! So he failed you? Most unfair. A low fellow."

"I was frightfully sick," said Gay.

Algy took a hand off the wheel to pat her shoulder.

"Bear up — there's always tomorrow. Avoid the scarlet pillar-box. But, my child, I seem to remember your saying you had a licence. How come?"

"Oh, that was Mummy's," said Gay brightly. "She left it behind when she went to Madeira."

"And you were going to take my unfortunate Bentley out on a fraudulent licence and ram pumps and pillar-boxes all over the Home Counties?"

"I mightn't have," said Gay.

"Ye gods!" Algy groaned. "And you call yourself a law-abiding citizen!"

"No, I don't. I think laws are silly — at least a lot of them are. I mean, if I wanted to break one I would."

Algy laughed.

"Come along then — what's your fancy in the way of a crime? I'd like to know."

Gay shivered, and didn't know why. Quite suddenly she felt like a lost dog and wanted to cry. It came over her that she might at this very moment have been trying to drive this large, strange car along a dark, strange road. She felt immeasurably grateful to Algy for having saved her from this. She said in a little melancholy voice,

"I might have man-slaughtered someone. It was very nice of you to come, because I should hate to be a man-slaughterer, and be prosecuted, and go to prison. And the family would foam, because they're all tangled up in a law-suit as it is, and it doesn't look as if it was ever going to end."

All this was behind them now. The darkness shut them in. Black, half-seen things slipped by — a big soft blur that was a house, and the long smudge that was a line of trees; water glinting for a moment and dissolving back into the gloom again. There is always a strangeness about driving at night. To have so small a visible space in which to move and yet to move so fast, to rush upon the dark and see it slide away, receding endlessly upon itself, induces an inertia of the faculties. Thought is in suspense, ready to move again when the spell is broken.

Gay had been in turmoil. She had been afraid, bold, eager, and afraid again. She had nerved herself to go down to Cole Lester. She would have nerved herself to the point of driving a strange Bentley along strange dark lanes. She would presently nerve herself to grope in a dark garden for Sylvia's blackmailer. Because Sylvia simply mustn't be allowed to hand over her husband's papers to Mr Zero, and the only way of stopping her that Gay could think of was to butt in at the critical moment and scare Mr Zero off the map. He was bound to be scared if he thought there was a witness to his blackmailing, and it ought to keep him quiet and prevent him from worrying Sylvia again. Gay had thought it a very good plan in London. Presently at Cole Lester she would probably not feel so sure about it. At the moment it was just a plan suspended between the time in which it had been conceived and the time at which it must be brought into action.

They came into Colebrook and stopped. One of the little bright yellow signs put up by the A.A. informed them that they had arrived. At a quarter before midnight there would certainly have been no one abroad to settle the question. The village was fast and dreamlessly asleep about its green, its pond, and its overgrown churchyard.

Algy said, "Well?" and waited. When there was no answer, he said, "What next?"

"I'm trying to think," said Gay.

She had been to Cole Lester once when Sylvia was engaged, but it was more than a year ago, and it had been daylight. She had to shut her eyes and call the daylight picture back. Mrs Thrale, and Marcia, and Sylvia and herself in the car which Francis had sent for them. Mrs Thrale twittering all the way. And they had gone on past the church and along a lane, and then there were big gates, big wrought-iron gates, and a stone pillar on either side with a thing like a pineapple on top. Mrs Thrale had given a sort of little gasp, and Marcia had chattered about what a lovely place it was, but Sylvia had just sat there and smiled without a word to say. Then Francis had met them and taken them all over the house, and the garden, and the grounds —

Gay opened her eyes and said,

"We turn up by the church — we've got to find the church."

"Church all present and correct," said Algy — "on the left."

"Then we turn up by it, and there's a lane, and you come to some big gates."

And suppose they were shut.

This thought, which might have occurred to Gay in town, bobbed up with horrid suddenness now. You simply can't take a blackmailer by surprise if you have to knock up a lodge and get yourself admitted in a flourish of trumpets.

The gates were open. Gay seemed to remember that the drive was a very long one. She wondered whether she dared let Algy drive her in. It would be nice to feel that he was somewhere near, and it would be very nice not to have to walk up that dark drive all by herself. But could she risk it? She didn't think she could, and when Algy said, "Do we drive in?" she made her voice as firm as possible and said, "No."

"What happens?"

"You stay here — I go in."

"Gay —"

"You said you wouldn't ask any questions."

"I'm not asking questions. But I don't like it. Why not tell me what it's all about?"

He heard an odd little laugh.

"Isn't that a question?"

"I suppose it is in a way, but not the way you meant. Look here, my dear, I'm not an absolute fool, and I can't very well drive you to Cole Lester without guessing —"

"You're not to guess. And I never said a word about Cole Lester, and — Algy, you *promised*."

"All right — my head's in a bag. I've never heard of Cole Lester — it's rather famous, you know — I don't

124

know that it belongs to Francis Colesborough, and I shouldn't dream of guessing."

"You're not to, you're not to! Oh, Algy, you *did* promise!"

"Yes — I was a fool. Well, I stay here. Are you going to be long?"

"I don't know," said Gay in rather a small voice.

"You'd better have a torch." He put it into her hand. "If I'm asleep when you get back, just wake me." He shut the door between them.

Gay looked at it with a horrid sinking feeling, and then turned away.

They had stopped just short of the gates, and Algy had switched off the headlights. She put on her little torch, found her way between the gateposts, and then put it out again. She must do without it if she possibly could, because her plan depended wholly on being able to get to the yew walk without being seen.

It was terribly black in the drive. She stood still and shut her eyes whilst she counted a hundred. When she opened them again she could see the black tracery of the trees against the sky, and the sky wasn't black — there was light coming through it, and she could see a star. She began to walk up the drive. Once or twice she blundered into a holly or a yew, but for the most part she was able to keep fairly straight, and as she went on her eyes began to see more and more. There was one blackness of a dense bush, and another of a tree. She kept a hand stretched out before her to save her face, but she didn't use the torch again.

In the end she came out upon the broad sweep in front of the house and could see it plainly as a great mass rising up against the sky. There was no light anywhere. The front seemed windowless, without a gleam. She stood at the edge of the trees and tried to think which way she must go. She had to get round to the back of the house. And there was a path — she remembered that there was a path.

She began to skirt the gravel sweep, keeping to the left, and presently she found what she was looking for. The path ran between shrubs. She had to use her torch once where two old hollies leaned together overhead, and once she thought she heard a footstep — someone moving, but she couldn't tell whether it was behind her or in front, or whether it was just the echo of her own footstep thrown back from the wall of the house. Her heart beat quick and frightened. She thought, "I don't know why I came. I can't stop Sylvia. I ought to have made her tell Francis. I can't do any good this way. Oh, I do wish Algy was here." But she went on, because even if a thing isn't any good, once you've started it you've got to see it through or else despise yourself for a spineless rabbit for ever and ever.

CHAPTER
SEVENTEEN

Sylvia heard the last stroke of twelve die away. There was an old clock against the end wall of the corridor, a tall old clock which struck with such a ringing sound that she could sometimes hear it in her sleep. Even after the sound had died away the air still seemed to tingle. There was a tremor now, and she waited for it to pass, because it frightened her a little. Everything frightened her a little tonight.

When the air was still again she opened a big mahogany wardrobe and took out a black satin cloak. She was still wearing the crepe dress which she had worn for dinner. She didn't very often wear black, but Francis liked it better than anything else, and she had wanted to please him. She had taken the papers out of his safe the night before. No one else could have done it. Francis never forgot his keys or left them about like other people did. But it had been quite easy for her to take them from under his pillow, and open the safe, and put them back again. She had found the papers at once, a bundle of letters marked Zero, so it was quite true what Mr Zero had said about the letters belonging to him, and of course Francis oughtn't to keep letters that belonged to someone else, but she did feel that perhaps she ought to be a little extra nice to him tonight. And the black dress would be quite good for meeting Mr Zero in. It wouldn't show any marks, and if she put on her cloak and pulled the hood up over her hair, no one could possibly see her as she crossed the lawn.

The letters were in her jewel-case. She lifted the lid. Francis had given her his mother's diamonds, but she didn't care for them very much. They really wanted setting again. He was obstinate about things like that. This room was frightful — all heavy Victorian mahogany, but she hadn't managed to move him the least little bit about it. She could get new chintzes if she liked. He wasn't going to have good old furniture turned out to make room for rubbish.

Under Lady Colesborough's diamonds in the bottom compartment of the massive old-fashioned case which had been Lady Colesborough's too the letters lay in a flat bundle. Sylvia had wrapped them in a silk handkerchief, an odd one of Marcia's, dark brown and green. She thought it very ugly and would be quite pleased to be rid of it. She put the packet in the pocket of her cloak, opened her bedroom door, and stood there listening. The servants were all in bed long ago, and Francis was in his study. He would be there for more than an hour yet, so that there was nothing to be afraid of. She had only to walk along the corridor and down the big staircase into the hall. She wouldn't even have to pass the study. It was quite easy. Yet she stood there for a long time hearing the faint, measured tick of the old clock. There was no other sound.

128

When she came to the stair head she listened again, but now she could not even hear the clock ticking. As she went downstairs, she thought of what she would say if Francis met her. He wouldn't of course, but if he did, what should she say? Biscuits — yes, that would do — she was hungry and thought she would like a biscuit. She wondered if anyone ever really ate biscuits in the middle of the night — so dry and crumby. Perhaps it had better be orange juice, or a book — but she hardly ever did read anything, and if Francis didn't believe her, it might be very frightening indeed. No, it had better be orange juice. Orange juice would be safe.

The hall was very large. The drawing-room lay on one side of it and the dining-room on the other, with the study behind the dining-room. There was no corresponding room on the other side, because the drawing-room took up the extra space, but there was a passage which ran past the drawing-room to a room that was called the Parlour. It was supposed to be Sylvia's own sitting-room, but she did not care for it very much. She would have liked to have the old dark panelling painted white and throw away the faded Persian rugs, but Francis would not hear of it. He said his mother had done her best to spoil the room by having a French window put in, and he wasn't going to let it go any farther.

It was the French window which was taking Sylvia to the Parlour. It opened so easily, and when it was open she would only have to cross the terrace and run down the steps to be straight in line for the yew walk. It was easy as easy, and if only Mr Zero was punctual, she would be back in her room in less than ten minutes. And what a relief that would be. —

Francis Colesborough pushed his chair a little farther back from the desk at which he had been writing. He had a letter in his hand, a letter which he had no more than begun to write. The last line was incomplete. He had the air of a man who has been disturbed, yet he himself could not have said what it was that had disturbed him. He stayed like that, listening, and heard a sound so faint that only a sense keyed to an unnatural tension would have caught it. It came to him as the sound of metal against metal, and immediately he remembered the window which had been unlatched two nights ago. He thought that someone had unlatched a window now. He threw the letter down upon the blotting-pad and went to the nearest window. With the curtains dropped behind him he looked out along the terrace and saw a bright rectangle aslant upon the flags. There was a light in the Parlour, and the curtains had been drawn back. The bright rectangle moved, the glass door swung. He had looked a half second too late to see who had opened it and come down the steps, but there was a shadow that slipped along the dark terrace and was gone. An open window two nights ago in town, and tonight an open door — and Sylvia slipping out — Sylvia —

He turned back into the room, pulled open a drawer, took out a small Browning pistol, and was back at the window, opening it before a tenth of a minute had gone by. He ran down the terrace steps and out on to the lawn. He was quicker than Sylvia and as silent. She did not know that he was no more than a dozen yards behind her as she groped her way into the black mouth of the yew alley. He halted there, and heard her going away from him between the over-arching yews. A twig broke now and then. He heard her catch her breath. The sounds receded.

He swung about and ran along the path which lay between the rose garden and the lawn. The path went straight to the end of the law, turned, and went straight again to skirt the yew hedge on the farther side and come out upon a stretch of level sward. Francis Colesborough came running by this way. He had no light, and needed none. These were paths he had trodden for nearly forty years. He had played at hide-and-seek about the old yew walk when he was a child of five. His foot knew every step and had no need for the guiding eye. He checked at the edge of the sward and moved out upon it, soft-foot and intent.

CHAPTER
EIGHTEEN

Gay came suddenly to the bushes' end and felt her feet on grass. The path had brought her out upon the wide lawn at the back of the house. She remembered it quite well. Francis had taken them out through a glass door, and first there had been a wide terrace, and then steps which led down to the lawn, and at the far end of the lawn a rose garden with the yew walk cutting it in two and spreading out like the top of the letter T to shut the roses in. So she had only to find the middle of the lawn and then keep straight on with her back to the house until she came to the open end of the yew walk.

She moved clear of the bushes and looked towards the house. She could see it very big, and blurred, and black, with the gloom of trees on either side of it melting away into the outer darkness. A little to one side a bright rectangle broke the shadowy mass. There was a door there, a door with glass in it right down to the ground, and there was a light in the room behind it. She thought that the door was open, and thought how exactly like Sylvia to come out at night on a quite dreadfully secret errand and leave an open door and a lighted room behind her.

132

She found her way across the lawn and came to the end of the grass. There was a path — she remembered that there was a path which bordered the rose garden, and Francis had told them how his father had made it when he cut down that part of the old yew hedge. "He had it cut because he wanted to see the roses from the house. Rather an old vandal." That was what Francis had said. And the cutting down had left the yew walk exactly like the letter T, with its long stem facing her now and the cross-piece running away to right and left on the far side of the rose garden.

Three steps took her over the path and into the black mouth of the walk. It was really a tunnel, for the yews met overhead, and had met and grown together and made an arching roof for hundreds and hundreds of years. It was quite pitch dark in the walk, quite, quite pitch dark, and dry under foot, with little brittle twigs and a queer cold smell. The walk was fifty yards long — Francis had told them so. She had to grope for fifty yards in the black tunnel where she couldn't see anything at all. But she ought to be able to make out the window at the far end. Because there was a window there, a wide rectangle cut in the hedge, and a seat where you could rest on a hot sunny day and look down a winding glade to the river and its meadowland.

She strained her eyes to find the window, and suddenly it sprang into view. A bright light flashed and was gone — flashed from the other side of the hedge and was gone. She saw nothing but the light — the sharp rectangle of the window and the light which made it visible. She heard a confusion of sound which she could not disentangle. She heard the sound of a shot, and she heard Sylvia scream. She began to run, with her heart pounding and her breath failing her. The picture of the lighted window floated upon the darkness. She ran towards it, and ran into the seat, bringing herself up with a bruising jerk.

The seat had a high oak back. She clung to it, steadying herself, and found the switch of her torch and turned it on. The beam shot straight ahead and showed her a bare arm, and a hand, and a pistol — a little black pistol — Sylvia's arm, Sylvia's hand.

Gay's wrist moved, and the beam went sliding up over Sylvia's shoulder to Sylvia's face. There was a black cloak over the shoulder. It had fallen away to leave the arm white and bare. She wished there had been something to cover Sylvia's face. It was quite white, quite terrified. It had a drowned look.

Gay said, "What is it?" but the words didn't make any sound. It was the most horrible thing that had ever happened to her, because she had said the words, and she said them again, and she tried to say, "Oh, Sylvia!" but there wasn't any sound at all. There hadn't been any sound since the shot and Sylvia's scream and her own heart beating hard.

Her hand wavered, and the beam came slanting down. She saw Sylvia open her hand and let the pistol fall. She heard it fall, and she heard the sound of someone running, and she heard Sylvia take a long, deep, sobbing breath.

She ran round the seat and leaned out through the window with her torch. There was a stretch of turf outside — a stretch of turf, and a man lying there with one arm over his breast and the other flung out wide upon the grass. The beam showed her Francis Colesborough's face, and she thought that he was dead. She felt cold, and stiff, and a little sick. She remembered the pistol that had been in Sylvia's hand.

She turned round and laid the torch on the arm of the seat. The pistol — she must find the pistol. Someone was coming — there had been a pistol in Sylvia's hand — she must find it — someone was calling her — someone was coming —

She held on to the seat because her knees were shaking, and stooped down to grope in the dry twigs and withered leaves. Her hand touched the pistol and found it, still warm from Sylvia's hand. This endless, dragged-out time had been only a moment, then. She stood up with the pistol in her hand and began to wipe it with the hem of her dress.

CHAPTER
NINETEEN

Algy had never had the slightest intention of allowing
Gay to go blinding off alone into dark, unknown
grounds with the fairly obvious intention of meeting an
anonymous blackmailer. She had, naturally, not
announced this as her reason for coming down here in
the middle of the night, but it seemed perfectly clear to
him that it was what she meant to do, and the minute
she mentioned Colebrook, and he guessed that their
destination was Cole Lester, he guessed too that it was
probably Sylvia Colesborough who was being blackmailed
and not Gay Hardwicke. He felt a queer rage against
Gay for getting herself mixed up with what was
probably a piece of crass folly and no business of hers.

As he followed Gay at a safe distance up the drive,
his rage turned back upon himself, because of all things
in the world he could least afford to mix himself up
with any new scandal. He was a fool to have come, and
a complete fool to have pledged himself not to ask any
questions. He ought to have insisted on asking them.
He ought at the very start to have said, "Nothing
doing" and hung up his receiver. He ought . . . In his
heart of hearts he knew perfectly well that he would

have taken Gay to Timbuctoo rather than let her run stupid risks without him.

He came to the end of the drive, and realized that he had lost her. What had he to do now? Follow the plan he had made and hope for the best. He wished her away — anywhere but here — in London — out of this business. It weighed darkly on his mind, darkly on them both. He went on . . .

As the sound of the shot rang out and died away, he began to run. A bird went up, startled, with a rush of wings. His torch was in his hand. When he came to the yew walk he switched it on and saw the dark mouth gaping. And then from the far end he caught the flash of another torch. He plunged into the tunnel and ran along it. He was more afraid than he had ever been in his life before. There was a nightmare sense of weight upon his feet and upon his heart.

He came to the seat, and the full beam of his torch shone across it and showed him Gay standing there with a pistol in one hand and a fold of her skirt in the other.

What he felt was not to be put into words — a blinding anger, a cold fear. What was she doing with the pistol — Gay — what had she done? He said her name, and she threw the pistol on the seat and came running to him helter-skelter like a child. She was in his arms and he was holding her before there was time for either of them to think or draw breath. He felt her strain against him, shuddering. All that had resisted her broke in him and dissolved. He said quick and low,

"What is it? Gay — darling — what is it?"

And Gay said, "He's dead! Oh, I think he's dead!"

"Who?"

"Francis."

"Where?"

"Outside — on the grass."

His arms tightened about her.

"Did you come to meet him? Was he blackmailing you?"

She put her hand against his chest and pushed him away.

"I can't breathe. Oh, *no* — it couldn't have been Francis — it couldn't!"

"Then why did you shoot him?"

"I didn't, I didn't, I didn't! Oh, Algy, I *didn't!*"

He released her.

"Where is he? Show me!"

They leaned together against the hedge and over the green sill of the window that was cut in it. In the light of Algy's torch Francis Colesborough lay dreadfully still.

"How does one get out there?" Algy's tone was almost matter-of-fact.

Gay looked away. Francis was dead. She was quite sure that Francis was dead. She pointed to the left and said in a small, faint voice,

"There's a way out along there."

There was, in fact, a way out at either end of the cross-piece. She didn't know why she had pointed to the left, but when he had run that way she thought perhaps it was because Sylvia had been standing on the right. He hadn't seen Sylvia — yet.

She picked up her own torch from the arm of the seat and flashed it round. Sylvia had been standing just there on the right of the window, but she wasn't there now. There wasn't anyone there.

Algy's voice called to her through the window, "Gay — come here," and when she came he leaned in across the sill and said,

"He's dead. Who shot him?"

She said nothing. Her mind was full of the dreadful picture of Sylvia with the pistol in her hand.

Algy caught her by the arm.

"Gay — if you did it, tell me. I'll get you away. Only for God's sake tell me!"

"I didn't! Algy, I *didn't!*"

"What were you doing with the pistol?"

"I picked it up. I was wiping it."

"Why? For God's sake, why?"

She burst into tears.

"I can't tell you. What are we going to do? Algy, what are we going to do?"

Question and answer had followed so fast that there had been no time to think, but now there was a most desperate need for thought. He said,

"I can get you away. We'd better chance it. Wipe that pistol again. Take hold of it with your dress. Don't leave any fingerprints. Then run along and meet me at the end of the hedge. If we can get to the car we can get clear."

Gay said, "You go. I can't." But what she really meant was, "If I go, that will put it on Sylvia. I can't leave Sylvia."

"Gay, if you did it —"
She stamped her foot.
"I didn't! I tell you I didn't!"
"Then we'd better go up to the house and get help."

CHAPTER
TWENTY

They did not need to go up to the house, for the house was roused. From the end of the lawn they could see lighted windows, black figures crossing them, lights moving, lights coming nearer.

"Algy, what are we going to say?"

"You came down to see Sylvia. I drove you. We heard the shot. We found him dead. Stick to it."

The lights came on. The butler arrived panting — a fat man, his face glistening with sweat in the light of a large electric lamp. He had a pair of trousers hastily pulled on. A striped pyjama jacket clung tightly. Gay remembered him, soft-voiced and decorous. He panted out,

"What are you doing here? What's up? What's happened? Her ladyship —"

"Your master's dead," said Algy. "He's been shot. You'll have to send for the police. And a doctor. My name is Somers, and this lady is Miss Hardwicke, Lady Colesborough's cousin. We were coming down here to see her. We heard the shot, and found Sir Francis lying on the grass beyond the yew hedge over there. I don't think there's any doubt about his being dead. We don't know who shot him. How many men have you got here?"

"There's two footmen, sir, and myself, and two men at the garage, and two gardeners who live on the place."

"Well, you'd better round them up. Someone must stay by the body and see it isn't touched. And put a man on any way into this tunnel place, because he was shot from there. The weapon's lying on the seat by the window. Hurry all you can. Miss Hardwicke will go to Lady Colesborough. I'll come with you if you like, but the police ought to be sent for at once. By the way, what's your name?"

"Sturrock, sir. Perhaps you'll get on to the telephone, sir. I'd best take charge out here."

"Where is Lady Colesborough? Miss Hardwicke had better tell her."

Gay caught her breath. Sturrock said, still panting,

"Her ladyship knows, sir. She came in running and calling for help. She roused us all, crying out that Sir Francis was shot. And then she dropped down in a faint, and the housekeeper's looking to her, and her own maid."

"Well, we'd better be getting along," said Algy.

Sylvia was in the study. They had carried her there and laid her on the leather-covered couch. She had come out of her faint and was sobbing hysterically, with her maid, a sensible-looking middle-aged woman, trying to soothe her, and the housekeeper, vast in pink flannelette and a waterproof, standing by.

Sylvia sat up when she saw Gay, clutched her, and said, sobbing,

"Is he dead? Oh, he isn't! Oh, he can't be! Oh, send everyone away!"

The two women went. Algy went. Gay heard him ask where there was another telephone, and then something about the butler's pantry. The door was shut. Sylvia stopped crying and said,

"Is Francis dead?"

"I think so."

"He shot him!" said Sylvia in a quick, excited voice. "Oh Gay, it was dreadful! They were quarrelling and he shot him!"

"Sylly — who?"

"Mr Zero," said Sylvia with a sob that almost choked the word.

"But you had the pistol in your hand — you had it."

Sylvia looked at her with wide, frightened eyes.

"I picked it up."

"But Francis was outside — the other side of the hedge. Where was this Zero man?"

"He was outside too."

"Then how did you get the pistol?"

Sylvia swayed as if she was going to faint again. She let go of Gay and said in a failing voice,

"I picked it up."

Gay caught her by the arm.

"Sylly, pull yourself together. You can't faint now — there isn't time — Algy is telephoning to the police. You've got to tell me what happened. You've got to make up your mind what you're going to say. They'll ask you hundreds of questions. Tell me what happened — quickly, before anyone comes."

Sylvia drew a long breath.

"I told you — I had to meet him —"

"This blackmailing Zero man?"

"Yes — I told you. I took the letters he wanted — out of the safe."

"Go on."

"I wrapped them up in a handkerchief that Marcia left behind. It was a very ugly one —"

"It doesn't matter about the handkerchief. Go on."

"It does, because that's why I couldn't find them — after I'd dropped them. I mean. It was a dark green handkerchief with a sort of brown check on it. I can't think why Marcia got it."

Gay thought, "It's exactly like a nightmare. Francis has been murdered, and we're talking about the colour of Marcia's handkerchief." She said,

"Tell me what happened — tell me what happened."

The couch was covered with crimson leather. Sylvia leaned back into the corner. Her black satin cloak had fallen open. The hood had dragged her hair and disarranged it. A bright spot of colour burned in either cheek. She said with a rush of words,

"Francis was here. I don't know how he knew I had gone out. I opened the parlour door —"

"You left the light on."

Sylvia looked faintly surprised.

"I never can remember about lights — I didn't mean to leave it on. I suppose Francis saw it."

"Sylly, you're not telling me what happened."

Sylvia began to breathe a little faster.

144

"I went right down to the end of the yew walk where the seat is, and the window, but I didn't like doing it a bit, because I don't really like that sort of place very much even in the daytime. I had a torch, and when I got to the window it shone through it, and Mr Zero said, 'Is that you?' and I said it was. And he said, 'Have you got those letters?' and I said, 'Yes.' And he said, 'Hand them over quick, and put out that torch of yours,' and I said, 'Why?' and he got awfully cross and said to put it out at once. And then we heard someone running, and it was Francis."

"How do you know it was Francis?"

Sylvia stared and shuddered.

"He called out. I was so frightened, I thought I was going to faint. Then they began to fight, and they were saying awful things. And Mr Zero said, 'Take that!' and there was a shot, and the pistol fell down and I picked it up."

Gay tried to think whether anyone would believe a story like this. She didn't see how they could. She tried to think whether she could believe it herself.

The door opened and Algy Somers came into the room.

She said, "Sylvia, will you say that all over again. To Algy. Algy's got to help us. You've got to tell him."

Sylvia turned lovely plaintive eyes on Algy and said it all over again. As far as Gay could tell she used exactly the same words, like a child repeating a lesson that it has learned by heart.

Algy brought a chair over to the couch and sat down quite close to them.

"Who is Mr Zero, Lady Colesborough?" he said.

Sylvia looked helpless.

"That's what he called himself when he talked to me on the telephone."

Algy said, "Yes?" in an encouraging voice, and, when that did not produce anything, "Don't you know his real name?"

"Oh, no," said Sylvia.

"You were meeting him to give him some letters. Will you tell me why?"

"He wanted them," said Sylvia with a sob. "He said they were his. He said he'd tell Francis — about the other things —" Her voice broke.

"He was blackmailing you?"

Two large tears rolled down Sylvia's cheeks.

"Yes, he was. And Gay said not to meet him, and I wish I hadn't now, but I didn't want him to tell Francis about the paper."

Algy said, "Help!" to himself. He had awful visions of the sort of witness that Sylvia was going to make, he had awful visions of what she might be going to say.

He asked, "What paper?" and with a complete sense of unreality heard Sylvia say,

"The one I took when I was staying with the Wessex-Gardners. I can't even remember the man's name."

It was Gay who said, "Lushington," and it was Gay who saw the white line come on either side of Algy's mouth. There was one of those silences which seem as if they might go on for ever. Then Gay put out a hand to stop Sylvia, and Algy said very quietly indeed,

"You took a paper from Mr Lushington's room at Wellings a week ago?"

"He made me," said Sylvia. "He said he'd give me two hundred pounds. And I'd lost it at cards, and Francis would have been so angry."

It seemed a complete explanation.

Algy said, "*He* being Mr Zero?"

Sylvia nodded.

"So I had to get the letters when he told me to."

Algy said, "I see." He got up and walked in the room. The window was open. Francis Colesborough had gone out that way. There was a drawer pulled out on one side of the writing-table, pulled out in a hurry and left. He stood looking down at it without touching anything. He wondered what had been taken from it in that last hurry, and saw a packet of cartridges lying there and thought, "It was his own pistol. He snatched it up and went out." There was a sheet of paper on the blotting-pad, a letter just begun. You don't read another man's letters, but Francis Colesborough was no longer another man. He was "the deceased" in a murder case, and one of the first things the police would do would be to read this letter.

Algy bent down and read it as it lay a little crookedly on the pale yellow blotting-paper.

There was no beginning. That halted him, because there was something strange in a letter which discarded all the usual forms. The strangeness sounded a warning bell. The check was momentary, yet in that moment he had braced himself against what might come. Without any change of expression he read:

"You disturb yourself unnecessarily. Neither Zero nor the agent is under the least suspicion. This rests in quite another quarter. M.L. has decided —"

The writing broke off there.

Algy Somers went back to the butler's pantry and rang up Montagu Lushington.

CHAPTER
TWENTY-ONE

Colonel Anstruther leaned back in his chair and frowned at Inspector Boyce. He had been a Chief Constable for ten years without ever coming to closer quarters with a *cause célèbre* than the pages of his daily newspaper. He now found himself threatened with a sensational publicity from which no man in the British Isles was more averse. He had an exact and orderly mind, and disapproved of crimes which could not be immediately docketed and pigeon-holed. He drummed on the arm of his chair and said,

"The Home Office is sending a man down. You'll have to take instructions from him as to the political issues involved. He will be present when the safe is opened, and so will Sir Francis Colesborough's lawyer."

"That was a very queer letter, sir," said Inspector Boyce.

"Damned queer. Damned treasonable, if you ask me. Home Office report on sabotage missing, Lady Colesborough confessing she took it under instructions from a blackmailer who calls himself Mr Zero, and her husband, who she thought was going to kill her if he found out, writing, 'Neither Zero nor the agent is under the least suspicion.' This means Francis Colesborough was in on that business, and lord knows what we shall find when we open his safe. 'Neither Zero nor the agent — ' Now suppose Francis Colesborough was Zero — the agent very probably his wife. They were staying at Wellings when the paper was missed. She's a pretty, silly woman. Suppose her husband put her on to getting the paper for him. Well, say she did it — what was she doing last night? She says — where's that statement of hers?" He plucked it angrily from the desk and leaned back again. "Yes, here we are. She says:

"'I went into the yew walk to meet a man who called himself Mr Zero. I have never seen him, and I do not know his real name. He said my husband was keeping some of his letters, and he induced me to take them out of the safe in our London house and bring them down to Cole Lester. He said they were his property and would have his name on them. I found a packet which was marked "Zero." It was this packet which I took into the yew walk. I did not take any pistol with me. I have fired a pistol, but I do not possess one. I am not a good shot. There is a window in the yew hedge. When I reached this window Mr Zero was there, but on the other side of the hedge and behind it so that I did not see him. He asked me whether I had the letters, and when I replied in the affirmative he told me to hand them over quickly. I heard my husband coming on the outside of the hedge to the left of the window. Mr Zero was on the right. They were both outside the hedge, and I was inside. My husband called out. He said angry things, and used language which I would rather not repeat. I don't remember whether Mr Zero said

150

anything then. They began to fight. I had a torch. I saw a pistol in my husband's hand. I think Mr Zero got it away from him. They were fighting just outside the window, and I was very frightened. I heard Mr Zero say, "Now what about it?" and, "Take that!" There was a shot. I don't know what happened to the letters. I don't know what happened to Mr Zero. I thought I was going to faint. I thought my husband was dead. I picked up the pistol — '"

Sylvia and the official mind had obviously collaborated. The result enraged Colonel Anstruther. He repeated the last sentence angrily.

"She says, 'I picked up the pistol.' What does she mean? What's the good of letting her make a statement like this? How could she pick it up if it was the other side of the hedge?"

Inspector Boyce gave a slight cough.

"She says it wasn't, sir."

"Wasn't what?"

"Wasn't on the other side of the hedge, sir."

Colonel Anstruther glared.

"Does she or doesn't she state that she was on the inside of the hedge and the two men on the outside?"

"Yes, sir."

"And that one of them had the pistol and the other got it from him?"

"Yes, sir."

"Then how the devil could she pick it up inside the hedge?"

"I don't know, sir."

"Then why didn't you ask her? If she says a thing like that she's got to explain it, hasn't she?"

Inspector Boyce stiffened and reverted to the extreme official manner.

"I did not omit to put that point to Lady Colesborough. She replied that she had no recollection of what occurred between the firing of the shot and the picking up of the pistol. If you will refer to the statement, sir —"

Colonel Anstruther referred to it with dislike. A most unsatisfactory document. He read in an annoyed voice:

" 'There was a shot. I don't know what happened to the letters. I don't know what happened to Mr Zero. I thought I was going to faint. I thought my husband was dead. I picked up the pistol — ' "

"Well, what about it? The pistol was outside, and she is inside, and she says she picked it up. What's the thickness of the hedge? I suppose you've measured it?"

"Six foot thick mostly, sir, but this window affair is cut in and there's not more than a four-foot thickness there."

"What's the size of the window?"

"Three foot high and six foot wide, sir. There's a seat inside, put facing it to get the view, if you understand. And there's this window, with a four-foot sill and the hedge jutting out beyond it on either side for a couple of feet. She says they were fighting just outside, but unless the man who had the pistol threw it in through the window after he had fired I don't see how it got the same side of the hedge as Lady Colesborough, or how she picked it up."

152

Colonel Anstruther looked up sharply.

"Is there any proof that there were two men on the other side of the hedge? Anything to substantiate Lady Colesborough's story of a fight?"

Inspector Boyce coughed.

"Dr Hammond says the pistol must have been at least a yard away from Sir Francis when the shot was fired. There aren't any footprints. It has been dry all day and the grass isn't marked. There's nothing to show whether there was a fight. There might have been someone there besides Sir Francis, or there mightn't. It all rests on Lady Colesborough's evidence. She says this man who calls himself Zero was there, and she says he fired the shot, but there isn't anyone else that saw him, and we can't find anyone that heard or saw a car."

Colonel Anstruther said, "Tcha!" and added, "What did you expect to find? People in Colebrook don't sit up at night counting cars, do they? I don't suppose anyone heard Mr Somers' car either, did they?"

"Well, no, sir, they didn't."

"Well then, what's the good of telling me nobody heard a car? That don't mean there wasn't a car to hear — does it?"

"No, sir. You asked if there was any evidence."

Colonel Anstruther made an explosive sound.

"And there isn't any! I take it there's no doubt that the weapon used was Colesborough's own pistol, because if there was another —"

"No doubt at all, sir. Sir Francis kept this pistol in a drawer on his writing-table — we found the drawer pulled out. He'd got a licence — all quite regular.

153

Sturrock the butler says there were a pair of them, but we haven't been able to find the other. It may be up at the London house."

Colonel Anstruther went back to the statement with a snort. He read aloud:

"'I picked up the pistol. I heard someone coming down the yew walk. It was my cousin, Miss Hardwicke. She came up to the seat. She had a torch. She came round the seat to look out of the window. I dropped the pistol and ran to the right along the hedge. There is a way out into the rose garden there. I went that way because I heard someone coming down the main walk and I was frightened. I ran to the house and rang the alarm bell in the hall. It rings in the servants' wing. I told them my husband has been shot. After that I fainted.'"

"This walk business," said Inspector Boyce — "I don't know if you've got it clear, sir. It's like a tunnel with the yews meeting overhead. There's a long straight piece with the rose garden on either side of it, say fifty yards, with a seat and a window at the end, and a cross-piece, say twenty yards, on either side, with an exit at both ends. Lady Colesborough went in down the main walk and came out on the right-hand side. Miss Hardwicke came in by the main walk and out the same way. Mr Somers came in by the main walk. It was him running in that Lady Colesborough heard. And he says he went out by the exit on the left-hand side and round outside the hedge to make sure of Sir Francis being dead, but he didn't touch him. Then, he says, he came back to Miss Hardwicke and they both returned by the main walk to the house, meeting the butler on the way. Mr Somers then telephoned the police. You've got their statements there."

"And what were Mr Somers and Miss Hardwicke doing in the grounds of Cole Lester in the middle of the night?" said Colonel Anstruther.

Inspector Boyce coughed.

"Mr Somers says he drove Miss Hardwicke down because she asked him to. He says he had never heard of Mr Zero, but, as one of Mr Montagu Lushington's secretaries, he was naturally aware that an important document had been stolen. He did not in any way connect the journey to Cole Lester with the stolen document. Miss Hardwicke says Lady Colesborough had confided in her that she was being blackmailed by someone she called Mr Zero. She asked Mr Somers to drive her down to Cole Lester because she knew that Lady Colesborough was to meet this man at the window in the yew hedge between twelve and one o'clock that night in order to hand over to him a packet of letters which she had taken from Sir Francis' private safe. Miss Hardwicke says she tried to persuade Lady Colesborough to inform her husband that she was being blackmailed, and having failed to do so, she hoped by being present as a witness to frighten the blackmailer and induce him to leave Lady Colesborough alone. I would like to say, sir, that in my opinion Miss Hardwicke is telling the truth."

"Well, she confirms Lady Colesborough's story to some extent. She says her cousin spoke to her about this Zero. She didn't see any signs of him last night — didn't hear anything?"

"Well, if you'll turn to her statement, sir —"

Colonel Anstruther put down the paper in his hand and took up another. His eye travelled down the page. He turned it and began to read aloud:

"'I had just got into the tunnel and began to grope my way along it. I had a torch, but I did not want to use it, so I was going slowly. I thought I ought to be able to see the window — '"

Colonel Anstruther looked up sharply.

"Miss Hardwicke is familiar with the grounds at Cole Lester?"

"She says she spent a day there with Lady Colesborough rather more than a year ago, before the marriage. She says she took a particular interest in this yew walk because she hadn't ever seen anything like it before."

Colonel Anstruther went on reading:

"'I thought I ought to be able to see the window. All at once I did see it, because there was a flash of light on the other side of the hedge. And I heard someone calling out. There was a lot of noise. I can't say whether there was two people shouting or only one. It was just a sudden noise which I wasn't expecting. I didn't hear any words, only this noise, and then a shot. After the shot I heard my cousin scream. I ran towards the window, and when I got to the seat I remembered my torch and turned it on. Lady Colesborough was standing there with the pistol in her hand — '"

Inspector Boyce coughed.

"She wasn't saying anything about the pistol till I showed her Lady Colesborough's statement."

Colonel Anstruther frowned. Boyce was too fond of the sound of his voice. He read in a repressive tone:

" 'I saw the pistol drop. I looked out of the window and saw Sir Francis lying there on the grass. He was about three yards away from the window. I thought he was dead. I heard someone running towards me down the tunnel. I picked up the pistol and wiped it on my dress. Mr Somers came — ' "

Colonel Anstruther said, "Tcha!" and struck his knee with the paper.

"Wiped the pistol, did she?" he rapped out.

"The pistol had certainly been wiped, sir. Mr Somers says she was wiping it when he came up. I think it is quite clear that Miss Hardwicke believed it was Lady Colesborough who had shot Sir Francis. I think that is quite certain. It suggests that she did not hear more than one man's voice. If she had got any impression that there were two men there quarrelling, she would not have suspected Lady Colesborough, and she would not have wiped the pistol."

"Nonsense!" said Colonel Anstruther. "You're talking as if young women are reasonable creatures. They're not. They don't reason at all. They don't think, except about their face-creams and their frocks. I've got three daughters and I know."

Inspector Boyce maintained a rigid decorum. Nobody but their father would have suspected the Misses Anstruther of devotion to frocks or face-creams. They were plain, meek women who did as they were told and left their faces as nature had most unfortunately made them.

"Well, she wiped the pistol. Any finger-marks left?"

"Nothing to speak of, sir."

"How do you mean, nothing to speak of?"

"She'd held it in a bit of her dress and wiped it as well as she could. She was quite frank about it — said she was frightened of leaving her own finger-prints. But she missed one low down on the butt. It's no value, because she's not denying she handled the pistol. It's a terrible pity she wiped it. We'd have known for certain whether this Zero was really there if she hadn't, and if we'd got a good print we might have roped him in."

"If you had wings you might fly!" growled Colonel Anstruther. "Lord, man — what sort of prints do you think you'd have got? If Lady Colesborough is telling the truth, there were four of them who handled it — Colesborough, Zero, herself, and Miss Hardwicke. You'd have been lucky to have got one straight print."

"We need a bit of luck," said Inspector Boyce.

CHAPTER
TWENTY-TWO

Every window in the study at Cole Lester was shut. The central heating was of a modern and highly efficient type. There was a blazing fire on the deep old-fashioned hearth. Sylvia Colesborough sat on one side of it in a leather-covered chair whose rich crimson threw up the gold of her hair and the pallor of her skin. She wore a thin black dress and an air of extreme fragility. Colonel Anstruther, who had perforce to occupy the seat on the other side of the fire, was being more painfully reminded every moment of a brief and unpleasant period of service in the tropics. His face was almost as red as the leather of his chair. The bald spot on the top of his head glistened. He mopped his brow. Even if the temperature had been some thirty degrees cooler, Sylvia's confidences might well have brought him to the verge of apoplexy. With Inspector Boyce sitting at Francis Colesborough's writing-table and taking notes, she had told the Chief Constable all about Mr Zero from the first telephone call. In a plaintive voice she had described the visit to Wellings, and what friends she and Poppy Wessex-Gardner were — "but Buffo's just a little bit dull, don't you think?" — and had then gone on with artless candour to explain how she had opened Mr Montagu Lushington's despatch-case and taken out the envelope which Mr Zero wanted. "And of course it doesn't sound a very nice thing to do, and I didn't like doing it a bit, but he said he'd tell Francis about my playing for money when he told me not to, and I was so frightened I'd have done anything, because, you know —" here Sylvia leaned forward a little and gazed at him earnestly — "because, you know, I'd lost five hundred pounds, and I can't think what he'd have said."

Colonel Anstruther could have said a good deal, but he restrained himself.

"Now, Lady Colesborough, will you tell me this? When did this Mr Zero give you the instructions about taking the envelope?"

A tiny line broke the whiteness of Sylvia's forehead.

"Well, it was on the Saturday — Saturday last week —"

"Yes, yes, but what time?"

Sylvia looked vague.

"Well, I'd had my tea — and I hadn't started for Wellings — because of course he couldn't have rung me up if I'd started, could he?"

Inspector Boyce covered his mouth with his hand for a moment. Colonel Anstruther's little fierce blue eyes looked as if they might at any moment pop right out of his head.

"So I expect it was about five," said Sylvia with a sigh.

Inspector Boyce made a note of the time. So did a quiet nondescript little man with sandy hair who was standing by one of the closed windows. His name was Brook, and he represented the Home Office, but so unobtrusively that it was difficult to remember that he was there at all. Sylvia had forgotten him long ago. For the most part he gazed abstractedly at the rain, and the wet grey terrace, and the wet green lawn. Sometimes he turned the same blank stare upon the room and its three occupants, sometimes he made a note. He made one now.

Colonel Anstruther blinked.

"And what time was it when you went into Mr Lushington's room and took the envelope?"

Sylvia leaned back again.

"I expect it was about half past seven — or eight — but I don't think it could really have been as late as that, because we were dining at a quarter past eight — because of Francis, you know. He told me to say he was afraid he was going to be late, and he *was* — we were half way through the fish, so I expect it was about a quarter to eight really. You see, I waited till I heard the bath water running."

Colonel Anstruther's complexion took on a livelier ruby.

"Bath water? Whose bath water?"

"Well, I *had* to wait till he was in his bath — I mean it wouldn't have been safe, would it?"

"Whose bath are you talking about, Lady Colesborough?"

Sylvia looked surprised.

"Mr Washington's."

Colonel Anstruther failed to repress a snort. He said in a military voice,

"Lushington, madam — *Lushington*."

"I never can remember his name," said Sylvia. "You see, Poppy and Buffo call him Tags."

Inspector Boyce's hand went up to his mouth again. He had a sense of humour, but he did not expect it to intrude upon a murder case. Colonel Anstruther was given up to whole-hearted wonder as to why, if murder was the order of the day, Lady Colesborough had escaped.

After an interval he proceeded.

"You say that you never saw Mr Zero."

"Oh, no. You see, it was always on the telephone or in the dark. And I met a man the other day who said that they were inventing something so that you could see people on the telephone, but I don't know that I want to really — because, I mean, you might be having your bath or anything, mightn't you?"

Inspector Boyce produced a very large white handkerchief and blew his nose. Colonel Anstruther raised his voice perceptibly.

"When you handed over the envelope which you had taken from Mr Lushington — Lady Colesborough, will you kindly give me your attention."

Sylvia fixed her eyes upon him with the expression of a docile child.

"Don't you see, madam, that anything you can tell us about this man is of extreme importance? You say it was dark and you did not see his face, but he took the envelope from you. Did you see his hand? I think you said he had a torch?"

"He had a glove on his hand," said Sylvia, unexpectedly lucid.

"What kind of a glove?"

"Oh, just a glove — the sort men wear — I expect you do yourself." Her lips parted in a small ingratiating smile which had no effect.

"Did you notice at what height the hand was?"

Sylvia looked blank.

"Don't you see, Lady Colesborough, that if the man was tall, the hand which he put out to take the envelope would have been at a higher level than if he had been short? Come over here, Boyce, for a minute." He turned his head. "And, Mr Brook — if you would be so good —"

The little man came over from his window. Superintendent Boyce looked down upon the top of a sandy head which barely reached his shoulder.

"Now," said Colonel Anstruther, "if you will each put out a hand, Lady Colesborough will be able to see what I mean."

Sylvia gazed earnestly, first at the tall, good-looking Inspector, and then at Mr Brook, that least noticeable of men. She said in a horrified voice,

"Do you mean that one of them is Mr Zero?"

Inspector Boyce very nearly disgraced himself. His face stiffened and assumed strange tints. Mr Brook remained unmoved. Colonel Anstruther said in the tone of a man who prays for patience without a great deal of hope that his prayer will be granted,

"Certainly not. I wish you to observe the difference in the height at which they are extending their hands. I want to know whether this suggests anything. Cast your mind back to the drive at Wellings. You gave that envelope to a man who put out his hand to receive it. Look at the Inspector, look at Mr Brook. Try and remember whether Mr Zero's hand was as high as the Inspector's or as low as Mr Brook's."

Sylvia looked, and said, "I don't know. But I'm sure he was tall."

"Why?"

"Because he was — I mean, I always thought of him that way — at least I don't know — I did then, but not afterwards."

"Excuse me, Colonel Anstruther —" said Mr Brook.

Colonel Anstruther nodded a, "That'll do, Boyce," and the Inspector went back to his notes.

Mr Brook brought up a small hard chair and sat down.

"Now, Lady Colesborough," he said in a soft, pleasant voice, "I want just to ask you one or two questions."

"I'm so tired of them," said Sylvia.

"I'm sure you are, but I just wondered what you meant when you said that at first you thought Mr Zero was tall but not afterwards."

Sylvia looked blank.

"I don't know — I just thought he was."

"You thought he was tall, and then you didn't think so?"

She brightened a little and said, "Yes."

"What happened to alter your impression? I mean, why did you think he was tall at first, and then stop thinking so?"

"Oh, but I didn't," said Sylvia a little breathlessly.

Mr Brook was of an admirable patience. He said,

"Will you try and tell me what you mean? It's very interesting, you know."

She smiled and relaxed. It was nice to feel interesting. She liked him much better than the old man with the red face. She really tried to remember.

"When he rang me up — you know, just before we went to Wellings — I thought — well, I thought it was wonderful of him to help me, because I was feeling as if I should die if Francis found out what a lot of money I'd lost, and it was all on the telephone, and I didn't notice about his being tall or anything like that, but when I gave him the envelope in the drive at Wellings he — somehow he frightened me, if you know what I mean."

"Yes, I know," said Mr Brook in his sympathetic voice. "Please go on, Lady Colesborough."

"I was dreadfully frightened," said Sylvia with a catch in her voice. "I ran all the way back to the house. That was the time I was sure he was tall. You know how it is — there's a sort of up in the air kind of feeling about the way they talk."

Mr Brook smiled encouragingly.

"I know exactly what you mean. You would have that feeling about the Inspector perhaps, but you wouldn't have it about me."

Sylvia looked pleased. She liked Mr Brook. The cross old man kept pretending not to understand what she meant, but Mr Brook knew at once. He had a nice soft voice too.

He said, "Then that was the first time you were actually in contact with Mr Zero, and you got an impression that he was tall?"

Sylvia's lovely eyes widened.

"Oh, no," she said.

"But, Lady Colesborough —"

"It wasn't the first time."

"Well, just for the moment I thought we would leave out the telephone conversation you had with him. I suppose that was really the first contact?"

The word puzzled Sylvia, but she said, "Oh, no" in quite a heartfelt way.

Colonel Anstruther's reaction was, "Well, he's getting it now. I wish him joy of her in the witness-box."

Mr Brook showed no sign of disturbance. He said gently,

"Tell me about the first time, will you?"

The little line which meant that Sylvia was puzzled showed for a moment just between her eyes.

"Do you mean the first time he telephoned?"

"The first time he did anything," said Mr Brook firmly.

"Oh, that was on a Friday, because I'd just been having my hair done — shampoo and set, you know."

"You remember it by that?"

166

"I always remember about my hair," said Sylvia in a reverential tone. "And he rang up and said he was so sorry — about my losing all that money, you know — and if I would meet him, he was quite sure something could be arranged."

"Did he say how he came to know you had lost this money?"

"Lots of people knew, but they wouldn't have told. It was at a party I went to with Poppy. I didn't know most of them."

"I see," said Mr Brook. "Let us get back to Mr Zero. He asked you to meet him. And did you?"

"Oh, yes, I did. We were coming down here, and he said if I met him just after twelve o'clock by the window in the yew walk —"

"Then last night was not the first time you had met him there?"

"Oh, no, it wasn't. And he said would I like to earn some money —"

"One moment, Lady Colesborough — when did he say this?"

Sylvia looked surprised.

"When I met him."

"I see. And that was down here at Cole Lester at midnight on Friday the twenty-ninth of January?"

"I suppose it was. He said such a lot of things, and it's so difficult to remember."

Mr Brook's voice was very persuasive.

"Try and remember just what happened when you met him — what he said — what impression he made on you."

"He said he wanted to help me, and he said would I like to earn a lot of money, and I said I would. And he said I could quite easily, and then he told me how."

"He knew you were going to Wellings?"

"Oh, yes."

"Did he mention Mr Lushington at that time?"

"I don't know. I suppose he did. Oh, yes, I know he did, because he seemed to think I ought to know about his being something in the Government."

"You didn't know Mr Lushington was Home Secretary?"

"I can't remember that sort of thing," said Sylvia in a helpless voice.

Mr Brook smiled at her.

"It's dull — isn't it? Now, Lady Colesborough, I'm not going to bother you any more, but I would just like to know what impression you got about Mr Zero the first time you met him by the window in the yew hedge."

"He was outside, and I was in — I didn't see him at all."

"He was outside, and you were in all the time, just as you were last night. Well now, how did he seem — all tall, and up in the air?"

"Oh, no, he didn't. I wasn't a bit frightened of him then."

"Thank you, Lady Colesborough. I don't think we need keep you now. I suppose your husband never mentioned Mr Zero to you, did he?"

Sylvia, glad to be gone, was already out of her chair. She said with unmistakable truthfulness,

"Oh, *no*. He didn't know anything about him. That was the only reason I did it — so that Francis shouldn't know."

CHAPTER
TWENTY-THREE

When the door had closed behind Sylvia Colonel Anstruther allowed his pent-up feelings to escape him.

"The woman's a half-wit!" he boomed. "I don't know what you thought you were getting out of her, Mr Brook. She can remember about her hair, but she can't remember when she made up her mind to steal papers from the Home Secretary. She can't put two sentences together without contradicting herself, and she can't give a rational answer to save her life."

Mr Brook looked up from making a note.

"An irritating witness, but not, I think, an untruthful one. An undeveloped mentality, and a childish outlook, but no deliberate attempt to pervert facts. One or two very useful points emerged from her evidence. She was not frightened of Mr Zero until she met him in the drive at Wellings. It was then that he began to strike her as tall and up in the air. I believe that was the only occasion on which his physical presence alarmed her. For the rest of the time she was afraid of his threats, of what he might do, and of her husband getting to know, but I don't think that he himself inspired her with any particular dread, or she would not so readily have agreed to meet him at the window of the house in town or in the yew walk down here. If she had been afraid she would have found a way out. She could have fainted, had hysterics, developed some fashionable complaint, or in the last resort have confessed to her husband. One thing is certain, she was much more afraid of Sir Francis Colesborough than she was of Mr Zero. I find this very suggestive, and one of the things it suggests is that the person to whom she handed Mr Lushington's papers in the drive at Wellings may very well have been Sir Francis himself."

Inspector Boyce lifted his head with a jerk. Colonel Anstruther said,

"Bless my soul, Mr Brook — that's a bit of a tall order!"

Mr Brook smiled his quiet, deferential smile.

"Not so tall, sir, if you will cast your mind back to the letter Sir Francis left behind him when he jumped out of that window to follow Lady Colesborough."

"You think he followed her?"

"I think there is no doubt about that. He was disturbed — that is obvious from the unfinished letter. He was very sharply and intimately disturbed or he would not have left a letter of this character lying open upon his table even for a few minutes in the middle of the night when he would not expect anyone to enter the room. I am certain that he heard Lady Colesborough open the parlour door. I have experimented with the bolt, and it is practically impossible to withdraw it without making a good deal of noise. I think Sir Francis heard this, saw Lady Colesborough across the terrace — she had left the light on and the door open behind her — and forgot everything in his desire to follow. He did not attempt to catch her up, but, having seen her enter the tunnel, skirted the rose garden and came up on the outside of the window in the yew hedge to the place where he was found shot. Now to return to the letter. You say it is a tall order to suppose that the man to whom Lady Colesborough handed the envelope in the drive at Wellings may have been Sir Francis. But consider that unfinished letter." Mr Brook turned the leaves of his notebook and read: " 'You disturb yourself unnecessarily. Neither Zero nor the agent is under the least suspicion. This rests in quite another quarter. M. L. has decided — ' Now, Colonel Anstruther, you will not dispute that this letter implicates Sir Francis up to the hilt. He is addressing an associate and assuring him that neither Zero nor the agent is under suspicion. Zero may be Sir Francis himself, or he may be this anonymous associate. The agent I take to be Lady Colesborough."

"Well, I agree about Lady Colesborough. I thought that myself."

Mr Brook resumed.

"I feel quite sure that Sir Francis was cognizant of Lady Colesborough's theft. As to his being Zero, I do not think that he would have risked speaking to her on the telephone — I think his associate did that — and I am quite sure he would not have risked meeting her and talking to her even on the darkest night. But I am inclined to believe that he received the papers from her in the drive at Wellings. For one thing, he was on the spot. He would only have had to leave the house for a very few minutes, and he had every opportunity of doing so. He and Lady Colesborough were the only two of the house-party who were not playing cards. You see, I have been on this case from the beginning, so I have a certain advantage."

"Quite so, quite so." Colonel Anstruther was obviously impressed. "Then you think that there were two of them, both calling themselves Zero?"

"I think Sir Francis was the moving spirit. Everything points to it. He was a man of dominating character. If he engaged in a criminal enterprise, it is unthinkable that he should be a subordinate, and the stake would have to be a big one to tempt him."

"But bless my soul, Mr Brook, the man must have known his wife was a fool. That's where I'm stuck. Would anyone in their senses have picked Lady Colesborough for a particularly delicate and dangerous job?"

Mr Brook nodded.

"I think so, Colonel Anstruther. I think it was a very clever choice. Who is going to suspect a lovely, charming, artless young woman who can hardly be said to have a mind at all? Even if she had been found in Mr Lushington's room, it would only have been supposed that she had mistaken it for her own. There are certain advantages in being a fool."

Colonel Anstruther said "Perhaps —" in a doubtful tone. "Then you believe Lady Colesborough's story? You believe she was meeting this associate of her husband's, and that it was he who shot Sir Francis?"

"We had better continue to call him Mr Zero. Yes, I think so. I think he was engaged in double-crossing his chief. He had induced Lady Colesborough to open her husband's safe and abstract a packet of letters."

"That is if you accept her story," said Colonel Anstruther. "We have only her word for all that. I'm not at all convinced that there was anyone else present when Colesborough was shot. Hang it all, she had the pistol in her hand. You can't rule out the possibility that she shot him herself."

"With what motive?" Mr Brook's tone was rather dry.

"One that you've supplied yourself. It's your own suggestion that Sir Francis was Mr Zero. Lady Colesborough goes to her assignation, taking the pistol with her, and shoots the man who is frightening her. She may have recognized him or she may not. She may have shot in a hurry and only discovered afterwards that she had killed her husband."

Mr Brook shook his head.

"I do not think so. I cannot believe that her assignation was with Sir Francis, first because I am quite sure that he would not have risked such a meeting and could have had no possible motive for it, and next because of the unfinished letter. If he had been planning to go out he would either have finished the letter first or put off writing it until afterwards."

Colonel Anstruther received this with scepticism.

"There may be something that we don't know about — unknown factor — there very often is. You make your theory, and something comes along and upsets it.

174

To my mind it's a perfectly plain case as far as the murder is concerned. The unknown factor is that we don't know what Lady Colesborough was up to. She may have been meeting someone or she may not, but I think Colesborough caught her out, and I think she shot him with his own pistol. The butler's evidence is that he kept it in an unlocked drawer, so she could have got it if she wanted to. And I say she did get it and she did shoot him. And there isn't a particle of evidence except her own to show that there was any other man there at the time — not a particle. And if Miss Hardwicke hadn't gone out of her way to wipe the pistol, we should have had a cast-iron case."

"Well," said Mr Brook, "I don't agree with you about there being no evidence, because it's an undisputed fact that Mr Somers was, if not there, at least very near at the time that the shot was fired. He says he was on the edge of the lawn at the point where the path comes out when he heard the shot. We have only his own word for that. He may have been nearer — he may have been very much nearer indeed."

Inspector Boyce's chair creaked as he shifted his weight. Colonel Anstruther said, "Bless my soul!" in an extremely startled voice.

"You see," said Mr Brook, "we have to consider what we know about Mr Zero. I believe Lady Colesborough was telling the truth when she described the various telephone conversations and the interview she had with him in the yew walk. At this interview, more than twelve hours before the report which was afterwards stolen had reached Mr Lushington, Mr Zero was

175

making his plans for having it stolen. He knew what it was and when it would be delivered."

"He couldn't have known that Mr Lushington would take it down to Wellings."

"Consider what he did know, Colonel Anstruther. He knew that Mr Lushington was going away. He knew that the report would be delivered to him before he went. I think we may assume that he knew Mr Lushington was in the habit of taking papers away with him. In any case, the last instructions were given to Lady Colesborough by telephone at five o'clock on the Saturday afternoon, some hours after Mr Lushington had left for Wellings with the report in his possession. It is quite certain that Mr Zero knew this. Now, in looking for Mr Zero, we have to look for someone who was in a position to know all these things. Mr Somers is in such a position. He is a member of Mr Lushington's staff and also of his family. He knew that the report was expected. He actually handled it and conveyed it to Mr Lushington. He had been under suspicion from the first, but at that time it was considered rather more than probable that the theft had taken place before Mr Lushington left town. Mr Somers had the opportunity of substituting the dummy envelope which was found when Mr Lushington opened his despatch-case. In fact, Mr Somers fills the bill very neatly. Perhaps he fills it a little too neatly — I don't know. Mr Lushington has complete confidence in him, but it is certain that Mr Somers knew about the visit to Wellings, that he knew about the report, and that he knew the report had been taken to Wellings. He could very easily have rung Lady

Colesborough up. There remains the damning fact that the man who knew these things was here in the grounds of Cole Lester at the hour of Lady Colesborough's appointment with Mr Zero, and at the moment when Sir Francis Colesborough was shot."

"Bless my soul!" said Colonel Anstruther in a tone of dismay.

Mr Brook got up and pressed the bell.

"I think we must ask Mr Somers to explain himself," he said.

CHAPTER
TWENTY-FOUR

Algy Somers came into the room, and found it hostile. Colonel Anstruther, grey of hair and red of face, was standing with his back to the fire. Inspector Boyce sat stiffly at the writing-table. Mr Brook, whom he knew by sight, looked up from a notebook and then down again. It was borne in upon Algy that he was here not only to be questioned, but also to show good reason why the suspicions of the occasion should not be focussed upon his person. It was a very disquieting impression. Colonel Anstruther's cold stare and Mr Brook's detachment did nothing to modify it. He could hardly sit while Colonel Anstruther remained standing, yet this position intensified the suggestion that he was in some sort a prisoner at the bar.

The Chief Constable opened the proceedings.

"I should be glad if you would repeat your account of what happened last night, Mr Somers."

"I have made a statement in writing, sir." Algy's tone was quiet and pleasant.

"You wish to adhere to that in every respect? Nothing you'd like to add to it?"

"Nothing that I can think of, but if there are any questions you would like to ask —"

Colonel Anstruther looked past him.

"Mr Somers' statement, Boyce."

The Inspector brought it over and went back to his seat. Colonel Anstruther frowned at the typewritten page.

"You say, Mr Somers, that Miss Hardwicke asked you to drive her down to Cole Lester. When was this?"

"Well, I was having a bath when she rang up — I suppose it was about seven o'clock. By the way, she didn't ask me to drive her to Cole Lester, she asked me to lend her my car. I wouldn't do that, but I offered to drive her, and she stipulated that I shouldn't ask where we were going."

"And when did you find out?" There was a sneering tone in Colonel Anstruther's voice.

A young man with political aspirations must learn to keep his temper. Algy kept his. He said,

"When Miss Hardwicke told me to make for a village called Colebrook, I guessed at once that she was going to Cole Lester to see her cousin."

"And you want us to believe that you asked no questions?"

"I had promised not to, sir."

"Perhaps you were going down to Cole Lester in any case?"

Algy allowed himself to be surprised.

"Oh, no, sir. My acquaintance with Lady Colesborough is very slight."

"Have you ever talked to her on the telephone?"

"Certainly not."

Mr Brook looked up.

"Did Miss Hardwicke give you any explanation of why she was going down to see her cousin in the middle of the night?"

"No, she didn't tell me anything."

"But you had your own ideas on the subject. Do you mind telling us what they were?"

Algy hesitated.

"It's rather difficult to say. I was a good deal concerned about Miss Hardwicke. She is very young, her people are abroad, and I had an idea that she was letting herself get mixed up in something that might — involve her in some unpleasantness. As soon as I guessed we were going to Cole Lester I thought it was something to do with Lady Colesborough. I had to let her go off into the grounds by herself, but I didn't feel at all happy about it, and as soon as I thought it was safe I followed her."

Colonel Anstruther returned to the statement.

"You say you followed Miss Hardwicke up the drive, and afterwards along the path that skirts the house. Did you know the place? Had you ever been there before?"

"No."

"Then how did you find your way?"

The question came at him sharply, but Algy took it with a smile.

"I had a torch, sir. I didn't use it more than I could help, because I didn't want Miss Hardwicke to know that I was following her."

"And you maintain that you followed Miss Hardwicke all the way?"

"Oh, yes — definitely."

180

Mr Brook spoke in his quiet voice.

"Taking into account the time that passed before you followed Miss Hardwicke, would it have been possible for you to reach the far side of the yew hedge by the time the shot was fired?"

"Oh, no — certainly not."

"But if a shorter time had elapsed — if you had followed Miss Hardwicke immediately, then it would have been possible?"

"No. I should still have been behind Miss Hardwicke, and she was certainly not more than half way down the tunnel when she heard the shot."

"Mr Somers, are you aware that the path which skirts the house divides at a point level with the terrace?"

"I know it now, but I knew nothing about it last night."

"Miss Hardwicke took the right fork and came out upon the lawn. If you had taken the left fork you would have passed the end of the yew hedge and come out upon the strip of grass behind the rose garden. You know that now, don't you?"

"Yes, I know it now."

"But you didn't know it last night?"

Algy's eyebrows went up.

"How could I know it? The place was utterly strange to me."

"You had never been there before?" The sneer was still in Colonel Anstruther's voice.

"No, I had never been there before."

Mr Brook took up the question.

"You had never met Lady Colesborough in these grounds?"

Algy smiled.

"I had met Lady Colesborough exactly three times before last night — twice at a night-club, the Ducks and Drakes, where she was with a party and I was with Miss Hardwicke, and once at the flat of some cousins of mine, the Westgates, where we dined at the same table and I afterwards talked to her for about ten minutes in the midst of a crowd of people. She told me that she adored London and hated the country. I can't remember anything else about the conversation."

"You haven't answered my question, Mr Somers."

"I thought I had. I had certainly never met Lady Colesborough either here or anywhere else, if by that you mean a clandestine meeting."

"And you have never been to Cole Lester before?"

"I have said so quite a number of times."

"But if you had been here before — if you were familiar with these grounds — you will agree that you could have reached the strip of grass beyond the yew hedge before the shot was fired?"

Algy smiled.

"I am not inclined to agree to a purely hypothetical case."

"Will you agree that a man who took the left fork would naturally outstrip anyone who, taking the right-hand turn, would have to find their way across the lawn to the entrance of the yew walk?"

"No, I don't agree at all. I should think that the distance would be about equal."

"But if the man who took the left-hand fork had a torch and used it, and if he ran, I think you will have to admit that he could have reached the place where the shot was fired in plenty of time to meet Sir Francis, snatch his pistol, and fire that shot."

"Well, I don't know that I'm admitting that either," said Algy. "Lady Colesborough says the man she went to meet was at the window in the yew hedge when she got there. She doesn't say anything about his coming up at a run and snatching the pistol. From what she told me, she and Mr Zero were talking through the window and she was handing over a packet of letters, when she heard someone running and Sir Francis arrived on the scene. Isn't that what she says in her statement?"

Mr Brook nodded.

"Sir Francis came from the right. He must have turned right at the path and skirted the rose garden in that direction. Anyone who followed the path which you and Miss Hardwicke took would have skirted the rose garden on the left and come out on to the grass on that side. Mr Zero would almost certainly have come that way, because it was the shortest and most direct route between the meeting-place and the road, where he would naturally have left a car. You did not observe any other car?"

Algy shook his head.

"There was no other car within range of my headlights. There may have been half a dozen farther up the road. I wasn't out looking for cars."

"Mr Somers, did you hear a car at any time either before the shot was fired or afterwards — especially afterwards? If Mr Zero did not remain at Cole Lester he must have got away — probably by car. Did you hear any car?"

Algy said, "Yes, I did," and thought how convenient a lie it must sound — 'If Mr Zero left Cole Lester, he must have left by car. Did you hear a car? — Yes, I did . . . ' It happened to be the truth, but there were times when you couldn't expect the truth to impose upon a child of five. He gave a short laugh and added, "You won't believe it, but it's perfectly true — I did hear a car, thought I didn't take any notice at the time. It was just before we met Sturrock and the servants. Miss Hardwicke may have heard it too."

Inspector Boyce turned in his chair. He addressed the Chief Constable.

"I put the question to her myself, sir, and she said she hadn't noticed anything. And the servants, they didn't notice anything either."

"They had plenty to think about," said Algy. "I didn't remember it myself until you asked me, but I'm quite prepared to swear to it now. I did hear a car, and it was going back the way we came."

"Suggesting that Mr Zero had run his car on a bit and left it turned all ready to go back to town again?" said Mr Brook.

Algy admitted a faint tone of sarcasm to his voice.

"I won't go so far as that — but then I haven't your imagination."

Mr Brook smiled faintly.

184

"Imagination may be very useful," he said. "Now I want to ask whether you noticed what time it was when Miss Hardwicke left you to find her way up the drive last night."

Algy had a sudden conviction that the answer to this question was going to matter a great deal. If he hadn't known the answer, it wouldn't have mattered. But he did know it, and it came home to him that if he gave it he might be landing himself in trouble, and if he hesitated it was bound to make a very bad impression. He said without any perceptible pause,

"I looked at the clock when Miss Hardwicke got out of the car, and it was just on twelve."

Colonel Anstruther said explosively, "What do you mean just on twelve, sir? Can't you be accurate?"

Algy looked in his direction. The old boy was hostile, definitely hostile. He made his voice as deferential as he could and apologized.

"I'm sorry, sir. It was between one and two minutes to twelve."

"Yes," said Mr Brook — "that is Miss Hardwicke's recollection also. How long did you wait before you followed her?"

"I gave her a couple of minutes."

"So you left the car at twelve o'clock. How long do you suppose it would take you to reach the strip of grass beyond the yew hedge?"

"I haven't timed it," said Algy. "I suppose you have."

Mr Brook nodded.

"It took me four and a half minutes this morning. I might take anything from five to seven or eight minutes in the dark. It might take no more than four for a man who had a torch — and knew his way — and was in a hurry to get there."

Algy laughed.

"In other words, you mean Mr Zero might have done it in four minutes. But then why should Mr Zero have been in a hurry?"

"We should be interested to know that," said Mr Brook. "Perhaps you will answer your own question."

Algy smiled.

"I'm afraid only Mr Zero could do that."

There was a momentary silence — rather a concentrated sort of silence. It said, with no need of words, "Well, here you are — the game's up. Why not make a clean breast of it?"

It would have given Algy the most extraordinary pleasure to take the Inspector by the scruff of his neck and bang his face on the table, chuck little Brook through the window, and let fly with the inkpot at old Anstruther. Instead he maintained an admirable self-control and waited for somebody else to speak.

The silence was broken by Mr Brook.

"Lady Colesborough says she heard the clock strike twelve just before she left her room. I have ascertained that this clock is five minutes fast. It was therefore six or seven minutes past twelve before she left the house. That would allow Mr Zero six or seven minutes to arrive at the rendezvous before she got there."

"But you don't know when Mr Zero started, or where he was coming from — do you?" said Algy.

"Don't we?" said Mr Brook. "I wonder. But we know when you started, Mr Somers. You could easily have reached the rendezvous before Lady Colesborough got there."

Algy contemplated him with amusement.

"I'm afraid that doesn't help you very much."

"No? Well, we shall see. Meanwhile here is a provisional timetable. 11.58, Miss Hardwicke enters the drive. 12 o'clock, Mr Somers enters the drive; Lady Colesborough prepares to leave her room. 12 to 12.05, Lady Colesborough leaves the house by the parlour door; Sir Francis follows her. 12.05, Mr Zero arrives at the rendezvous. 12.07, Lady Colesborough arrives at the rendezvous. 12.08 to 12.09, Sir Francis gets there after skirting the rose garden. 12.10, Sir Francis is shot. 12.11, Miss Hardwicke arrives and finds Lady Colesborough holding the pistol. The butler Sturrock says it was just after a quarter past twelve when the alarm-bell rang and aroused the servants' wing."

"Quite so," said Algy. "May I point out, however, that your timetable rests chiefly on guesswork? Miss Hardwicke and I can corroborate each other as to the time she left the car, and Sturrock's evidence as to the time the alarm-bell rang probably has the support of the rest of the staff, but between 12 and 12.15 you're just guessing, and you know it. It's no use asking anyone who has ever met Lady Colesborough to expect her to be accurate about time. If she said she heard a clock strike just before she left her room, it might have been one minute before or it might have been ten — I don't suppose she'd notice the difference." He turned to Colonel Anstruther. "You've been talking to her, sir. Would you expect her to be accurate — well, about anything?"

"Woman's a half-wit," said Colonel Anstruther. "Waste of time talking to her — waste of time asking her anything. Hasn't got a mind, and doesn't try to use whatever it is she's got instead. I'll give you that if it's any use to you, Mr Somers — you'll want all you can get. Any more questions, Mr Brook?"

Mr Brook shook his head.

CHAPTER
TWENTY-FIVE

"When are we going to get away from this horrible place?" said Gay.

She and Algy Somers were standing side by side, looking out from the drawing-room across the terrace and the lawn to the rose garden divided and enclosed by the dark T shape of the yew walk. There were five windows, straight and rather narrow, all hung with curtains of pale, cold brocade which repeated the faded green of the winter grass and the grey and blue of the winter sky. Gay and Algy were at the middle window, standing close but not looking at one another. They looked instead at the lawn where they had groped in the dark, and the black mouth of the tunnel down which they had run to find a murdered man.

"When are we going to get away from this horrible place, Algy?"

Algy smiled.

"I don't know, my child — when they've made up their minds whether to arrest me at once or to wait for the inquest. You'll have to stay for the inquest anyhow, I'm afraid, but you'll be able to go as soon as it's over. If I'm not figuring as the accused by then, I shall be able to go too — we might even go together."

Gay swung round with a bright colour in her cheeks. "They don't — they can't!"

Algy saw the colour out of the tail of his eye, and avoided looking at it.

"Oh, they're quite sure that I am Mr Zero, and that I shot Sir Francis. The only thing they're not sure about is whether they've got enough evidence to put before a jury. I don't think they have myself, but if they do, they'll be three to one, and I shall be for it."

Gay's hand kept slipping inside his arm, tugging at his sleeve.

"Don't! Don't say it! Algy, please don't say it."

He was aware of her looking over her shoulder as if she expected the immediate entry of the Inspector. He turned to her then with half a laugh.

"They'll wait till the safe has been opened anyhow. Mr Patterson, the Colesborough family solicitor, is coming down to be present. Stuffy old boy. Furious at being called out on a Sunday, and ready to have apoplexy at the idea of their proceeding without him. I could hear old Anstruther fairly booming at him on the telephone — and getting as good as he gave, I should say. I was the other side of the hall or I might have heard Patterson too. The study door was ajar and they were at it hammer and tongs. In the upshot, I gathered that Patterson would be here in time for tea — another jolly, companionable meal."

Gay's hand was warm against his arm, against his side. It shook a little as she said,

"What's in the safe?"

"Something that'll show them I'm not Mr Zero, I hope, but you never can tell."

"If there's anything, it'll be here," said Gay. "Sylvia swears there weren't any papers in the town safe, only the packet of letters she took. I told them that, and they asked her and she stuck to it. So if there's anything to find, it'll be here."

"Monty will probably blow in some time," said Algy. "He's staying with the other Wessex-Gardner, the one they call Binks, only about five miles from here. Maud Lushington and Constance Wessex-Gardner are sisters." He laughed a little. "He takes the wretched Brewster down and makes him work like a galley slave. The funny thing is that Brewster likes it. He told me once in a hushed voice that it was a privilege which he appreciated very highly, and he rather gave me up as a lost soul when I said he could keep it as far as I was concerned. Of course he's the perfect secretary and I'm not. I'd much rather be doing something on my own."

Gay's hand pulled at his arm.

"Algy — will Mr Lushington stand up for you?"

"He's been a brick so far, but — well, he's got to be careful. If I wasn't his cousin, it would make it a lot easier for him to take my part."

Gay pressed closer.

"It's going to be all right. Algy, say it's going to be all right!"

Algy looked out at the yew walk.

"It's going to be as right as rain, my dear."

"Then why won't you look at me?"

"Because I think I'd better not, Gay."

She said, "Why?" and only just managed to get the word to make any sound at all. The sound was so small that Algy did not feel obligated to take any notice of it. He made instead a movement to release himself, but in doing so he found Gay's upturned face much, much nearer than he expected. It was on a level with his shoulder, the eyes very bright and intent, cheeks glowing and lips just parted on that trembling word. They looked at one another, and he said,

"My dear — I mustn't — now —"

Gay said, "Why?" again. This time it was only a breath like a sigh, but it came from her very heart. She had both hands clasped about his arm, and he was trying to unclasp them. He said,

"You know why."

"I don't care," said Gay. "I don't care a bit what anyone thinks, and I don't care if they arrest you." Her hands clung to each other and to him. "I don't care about anything unless — unless you don't care for me."

There was a dreadful little pause. Her clasp relaxed. She stepped back, her eyes suddenly blurred so much that she couldn't see, and in a forlorn and faltering tone she said,

"You don't. It — it doesn't matter if you don't, Algy."

She felt her left hand caught, and blinked away two blinding tears. Having got her hand, Algy was holding it so tight that it felt as if all the bones were breaking. This was naturally very encouraging, but just as she managed to swallow a sob that was threatening to choke her the comforting pressure ceased. She had her hand again, rather the worse for wear, and Algy Somers had reached the door and banged it behind him.

Gay dried her eyes, and presently went upstairs to Sylvia.

CHAPTER
TWENTY-SIX

Sylvia was lying on the old-fashioned couch in her room. She looked pale and depressed, but she brightened up when Gay came in.

"Are they still asking everybody questions?" she said in a plaintive voice. "They do ask a lot, don't they? I'm sure they went on and on at me until I felt quite giddy. Will they go away soon, do you think?"

"I don't know," said Gay. Her heart felt like a heavy stone inside her and her throat was dry. She would have liked to put her head down in Sylvia's lap and weep, but you couldn't do that sort of thing.

Sylvia sighed.

"It would be nice if they would go away, wouldn't it? I don't mind Algy — he's nice, but I wish the Inspector would go away, and that Mr Brook, and Colonel Anstruther. Why did they want to ask me all those questions? It isn't as if they could possibly think that I shot Francis." She shivered, and her voice had a frightened sound. "They *couldn't* think that — Gay, they couldn't!" They kept wanting to know why I picked up the pistol. And I *don't* know. It was all so quick and so dreadful. But they can't think I did it.

Why, you were there, and Algy. Why couldn't it have been Algy?"

"Sylvia!"

"I mean, why don't they think it was Algy?"

"They do," said Gay, and felt a cold breath of terror touch her and go past.

Sylvia said, "Oh," and then, "What a good thing."

"*Sylvia!*"

A little colour had come into Sylvia's cheeks.

"You needn't say, '*Sylvia!*' like that. I mean, if they think it was Algy they won't go on thinking it was me, will they, darling? And then they won't go on asking me all those silly questions."

Bright anger looked out of Gay's eyes, but it faded again. What was the good of being angry? It never had been any use with Sylvia. She said,

"Sylly, don't you truly remember how you came to have the pistol? Let's go over it together and see if it doesn't come back to you. What was the first thing that happened when you got to the window in the hedge?"

"I had my torch," said Sylvia, "and the light went through the window, and Mr Zero said, 'Is that you?' and I said, 'Yes.' And he said, 'Have you got those letters?' and I said I had, and he asked if I'd looked at them and I said of course I hadn't. I mean, why should I — horrid things. But he went on about was I sure I hadn't, and I said, 'Don't be silly.' And then he said, 'Hand them over quick and put out that torch!' I think he said 'that damned torch.' And I wanted to know why, and he got angry and said, 'Put it out at once, I tell you!' And then Francis came running, and there was a fight, and the pistol went off and I picked it up."

"Sylly, how could you pick it up when they were on one side of the hedge and you were on the other?"

Sylvia stared with those blue eyes of hers.

"He shot Francis, and he threw it down and I picked it up."

"You mean he threw it in at the window? Is that what you mean?"

"I suppose so," said Sylvia in a helpless voice. "Yes, that's what he must have done, because something hit my shoulder and made a bruise there. I expect it was the pistol."

"Did you tell Colonel Anstruther that?"

"Oh, no darling," said Sylvia. "I've only just thought about it myself."

"You must tell him," said Gay. "Now, Sylly — think! What happened to the letters?"

"I don't know, darling."

"Just think. Did you give them to Mr Zero? You say he told you to, but did you do it? Did you?"

"I don't know, darling — at least —"

"Good girl — go on."

Sylvia looked puzzled.

"If I'd given them to him I wouldn't remember crunching them up in my hand when they were fighting, would I?"

"I shouldn't think so. Is that what you remember?"

Sylvia's voice had a groping sound.

"Well, I did think so — just now — when you asked me — but I don't know really — I just had the sort of feeling of the corners running into my hand —" She gazed at her open palms as if she expected to find the mark of the stolen letter there.

"But Sylly —"

The telephone bell rang from the table beside the big four-post bed. Sylvia got up as if she were glad of the interruption. She put the receiver to her ear, and heard a voice which set her heart knocking against her side.

"You know who is speaking, Lady Colesborough."

Sylvia said, "Do I?" And then panic took her, and she added in a choking hurry, "Yes, yes, yes — of course I do. What do you want?"

The voice said, "I want those letters. Where are they?"

"I don't know. Everyone asks me that, and I don't know."

"The police haven't got them?" Mr Zero's voice was smooth, but there was a sound in it as if the smoothness might break — quite suddenly, at any moment.

Sylvia said, "Oh, *no*. Oh, I'm sure they haven't, because they keep asking me — everyone does."

"And what do you say?"

"I don't know," said Sylvia. "I mean, that's what I say, but I *don't* know."

"Keep right on saying it," said Mr Zero, and rang off.

Sylvia, turning round with an expression of relief, was met by a demanding look from Gay and a quick "What was that?" The relief faded.

197

"He wanted to know about the letters too. I told him I didn't know."

"Sylly, who was it? Who were you speaking to? Who asked you about the letters?"

"It was Mr Zero," said Sylvia. Her voice began confidently and then shook. It shook most on the name.

"Mr Zero!"

Sylvia caught her breath in something like a sob.

"He oughtn't to, ought he? Not if he shot Francis. I don't think he ought to ring me up like that."

Gay had a startled look.

"You ought to tell them at once. They ought to find out where the call came from."

But Sylvia shook her head.

"Oh, no," she said.

"Sylly!"

"He wouldn't like it at all," said Sylvia with conviction.

Gay looked, opened her mouth to speak, shut it again, and ran out of the room. What was the good of speaking to Sylvia?

She ran all the way downstairs and into the study. The three men who were there all turned to look at her. Inspector Boyce admired the scarlet in her cheeks and the sparkle in her eyes. Mr Brook wondered what had brought her there in such a flying hurry. Colonel Anstruther was confirmed in his convictions that girls had no manners nowadays.

Gay stood with the open door in her hand and said, with the words tripping over each other,

"He's just called her up! He's been talking to her — on the telephone — Mr Zero! So it couldn't be Algy — you *must* see that it couldn't be Algy if he's just been talking to Sylvia on the telephone!"

Colonel Anstruther said, "Bless my soul!" and Mr Brook said, "Won't you please come in and shut the door, Miss Hardwicke, and sit down and tell us what you mean?"

She came in, and the door fell to with a bang.

"You must see that it can't be Algy now!"

Mr Brook said, "Why?" and looked at her.

She stamped an angry foot.

"Didn't you hear what I said? Or are you all too stupid to take it in? I tell you Mr Zero rang up — just now, just this minute, while I was up in Sylvia's room. He wanted to know about the letters. So how could he be Algy? Algy couldn't be telephoning to Sylvia — you must see that. Algy's in the house."

Colonel Anstruther said, "Tcha!" and would have gone on to say something else, but Mr Brook was before him.

"Mr Somers went out in his car about twenty minutes ago," he said.

CHAPTER
TWENTY-SEVEN

When Algy left Gay in the drawing-room he went straight down to the stables and got out the Bentley, which had been consigned to a coach-house. He wondered whether anyone would stop him. Hardly, at this juncture — unless they were prepared to arrest him then and there. No, he fancied that they wouldn't do that — not till the safe had been opened at any rate. His own feeling was that if he stayed in the house another minute he would find himself telling Gay just what he thought of her, or old Anstruther just what he thought of him, and he didn't want to do either. He wanted to get on a straight road and let the Bentley out.

He emerged upon the lane, turned right-handed, and was aware of a plodding figure head, a figure in a dark blue suit and a bowler hat, not at all the figure of a man who walks for pleasure in the muddy lane. Algy recognized Sturrock the butler, wondered where he was off to, and then remembered that this was Sunday afternoon. It was probably Sturrock's afternoon out, and the fact that his master had been shot last night was not, apparently, to interfere with his taking it. On an impulse Algy slowed down as he passed, opened the door on the butler's side, and said,

"Like a lift, Sturrock?"

The man stood still. He had an egg-shaped face, pale and smoothly shaved. His manner was respectful as he said,

"I should be very much obliged, if it wouldn't be troubling you, sir."

His voice suggested that he served a house in mourning — a rich voice, with a kind of funeral hush upon it. Algy didn't like it very much — or him. He was short, "No trouble at all — jump in," and shut his own door again.

At any time in the past fifteen years it would have been impossible for Sturrock to jump. He climbed in at the back and closed the door noiselessly behind him. A man of weight, a man of dignity, a man who certainly would not walk for choice. Algy wondered where he was bound for, and said without turning round,

"Well, where can I drop you? Colebrook?"

"If you are not going any farther, sir."

"Railing any good to you?"

"I shall be very grateful, sir. I was afraid I might have missed the bus, but I shall get one back all right. It's my half day, and there seemed no reason why I should stay in. I mentioned it to the Inspector."

"I'm afraid I didn't," said Algy.

Sturrock pursued the subject in an earnest, painstaking manner.

"The Inspector said it would be quite all right, sir. But I shall not be taking the full time. There is a bus at half past four — I thought of catching that. I shall be in the house again before five o'clock. I told the Inspector that such was my intention. I told him I shouldn't feel comfortable about being out of the house for long — not in the circumstances. William has only been there a short time, and, as I said to the Inspector, if there was to be any emergency it would be beyond him, especially after last night."

Algy was profoundly bored with Sturrock's scruples. Railing was, mercifully, only four miles away. He dropped the butler in the market-place, and as he drove out of the square on the farther side, his driving mirror showed him a blue suit and bowler hat disappearing within the doors of the Hand and Flower. If the walls had been transparent, he would presently have seen them esconced within a telephone booth, the bowler hat a thought pushed back, the eyes beneath its brim intent, watchful, and aware.

Algy Somers got back to Cole Lester at half past four. Mr Patterson, Sir Francis Colesborough's solicitor, had arrived, and the business of opening the safe was going forward in the study behind closed doors. It fell therefore to Algy to receive Mr Montagu Lushington when he arrived at about a quarter to five. He had Mr Brewster with him, and explained that they were on their way back to town — "And I must say, Algy, that you have a singular knack of getting into the limelight. Why you must needs get yourself mixed up in a murder case at this juncture! Heaven knows there's enough talk already. I'll see Brook, but things will just have to take their course. Maud is staying on with her sister for a day or two, so I'm taking Brewster back with me. I hope Lady Colesborough won't think we're intruding. I suppose she is keeping to her room."

Algy very nearly said, "Lady Colesborough doesn't think," but pulled himself up in time. It seemed rather difficult to find the right thing to say. If Brewster hadn't been there, he could have talked freely to Monty, but there was Brewster, a little embarrassed, a little shocked, and obviously just a little thrilled at finding himself in the midst of a case which would be front page news in every paper in the country tomorrow, and actually shaking hands with the principal suspect.

Algy said he didn't think Sylvia would come down. He supposed that someone would bring them some tea. They were in the drawing-room, and to the drawing-room upon the stroke of five tea was borne processionally by Sturrock and two attendant footmen. Algy thought the butler had cut his afternoon uncommon short. He ventured a, "Got your bus all right, Sturrock," and received a glance of dignified rebuke and a quiet, "Yes, thank you, sir."

Neither Gay nor Sylvia appeared, but presently Colonel Anstruther and Mr Patterson came in, from which Algy deduced that the business of clearing the safe had been despatched. If he expected any information he was disappointed. Colonel Anstruther drank several cups of tea all scalding hot, and half emptied the sugar-basin without perceptibly sweetening his temper. He also partook of buttered toast, scones, and three slices of chocolate cake. These exertions left no room for conversation. He ate, he drank, he appeared to be on the point of saying, "Tcha!" several times, and he regarded Mr Brewster's painstaking endeavours to make conversation with warm dislike. Mr Patterson, who only drank hot water and refused food rather as if he suspected it of being poisoned, was quite as uncommunicative. Algy thought he had never seen an elderly gentleman in a worse temper.

Monty discoursed upon migratory birds, a perfectly safe subject in which no one took any interest except Cyril Brewster, who, like a dutiful acolyte, supplied at intervals such responses as, "How wonderful!" and, "Marvellous indeed!" Not one of those meals which lend gaiety to social life.

There was a moment when Mr Patterson broke his ferocious silence to observe that the country was an unendurable place in winter and it passed his comprehension how any civilized man could endure it. "Barbarous — completely barbarous," he said, and reverted to sipping hot water.

There was a moment when Mr Brewster, in a desire to make harmless conversation, addressed himself with an air of diffidence to the company at large.

"It's a pity that the evenings are still so dark. If it had been lighter, I should have been so much interested in seeing the grounds. There is a famous yew hedge, is there not?"

Colonel Anstruther brought out a most undoubted, "Tcha!" Fellow was a secretary, wasn't he? In his young days secretaries spoke when they were spoken to.

Algy gazed almost reverentially at the unconscious Cyril.

"There is certainly a yew hedge," he murmured. "Oh, my only aunt!"

"You mean?" Mr Brewster raised anxious eyebrows.

"Oh lord, *yes*, man! That's where Colesborough was shot!"

"Indeed — I had no idea." The embarrassed tone faded out.

Montagu Lushington went on talking about birds.

It was over at last. Colonel Anstruther and Mr Patterson withdrew, presumably to the study. Mr Lushington expressed a wish to see Mr Brook, who presently appeared. Algy Somers and Cyril Brewster left the room.

CHAPTER
TWENTY-EIGHT

The door of the butler's pantry opened and Mr Zero came in. He shut the door behind him and said in an easy, affable voice,

"Well, Sturrock, have you got them?"

Sturrock had turned round at the first sound, but he showed no surprise. He was expecting Mr Zero, and expecting to make a very good thing out of him. There would be some haggling and chaffering, but he wasn't going to come down in his price. He had the letters, and that was all the same as having Mr Zero's neck in a noose. What a bit of luck — what a really remarkable bit of luck his being first down to the yew walk. They had all come streaming away without so much as a thought for the letters and left him to find them where they had dropped, right down beside the hedge, under the window. Well, he'd got them cheap and he meant to sell them dear, and he didn't mean to run any risks neither. No meetings in dark gardens for him, not if he knew it. If Mr Zero wanted to talk, he could do it here where he wouldn't be tempted to try any more of his fancy stuff. All this took no time. It was in his mind, a settled policy, all thought out and clear. He didn't have to think about it. So when Mr Zero said, "Have you got them?" he had his answer ready.

"I've got them all right, if you've got the money, sir."

"Fair exchange," said Mr Zero. Then he looked across at the other door. "How private are we? What's through there?"

Sturrock glanced over his shoulder.

"Private enough," he said. "No one comes eavesdropping on me. There's a passage between this and the servants' hall, and they've got the wireless on there — military band programme. We're private enough. Have you got the money?"

"I have got it," said Mr Zero. He put a hand in his pocket and pulled out a wad of notes. "Lucky I had them by me — for emergencies. You never know, do you? Quick, man — show me the letters!"

Sturrock's eyes were on the notes. Money for jam, that's what it was — big money, and not the last of it neither, because as long as he knew what he knew he could cut and come again. As long as he knew . . . He dived into an inside pocket and brought out a knotted green silk handkerchief checked with brown. It had been untied, and tied again, since Sylvia Colesborough had fastened the stolen letters in it, and the knots were loose and slipping. Sturrock pulled out the letters — there were no more than three of them — and pushed the handkerchief back into his pocket. He'd burn it presently. It would be better burned. It was the letters that were worth their weight in gold — and more.

Mr Zero threw the bundle of notes down upon the *News of the World* which lay spread out on the pantry table.

"Count them while I have a look at the letters," he said. He stretched out his left hand for them.

The butler hesitated, leaned forward, reached for the notes, and saw Mr Zero's right hand go down into his pocket again — a gloved right hand.

But it hadn't been gloved just now —

Mr Zero smiled, took a long step forward, and shot him dead.

There was very little noise. The pistol had been fitted with a silencer. This Mr Zero removed.

Sturrock had fallen across the table, but the heavy body would probably slide down on to the floor. With his gloved hand Mr Zero clasped the limp right hand about the pistol butt. He put the letters and the notes into his pocket. Then he left the room.

William gave the alarm ten minutes later, rushing white-faced into the study.

"Mr Sturrock — oh, sir, he's shot himself! Oh, sir!" And then an incoherent story of how he had tried the door of the butler's pantry, the one on the kitchen side, and found it locked — "And when I couldn't get an answer I went round by the other door — and he's shot himself! Oh, sir, whatever made him do it!"

Inspector Boyce went quickly out of the room. The study faced the terrace, with the dining-room behind it, and the butler's pantry behind that. As he ran through the hall, he saw Algy Somers on his way downstairs. He ran on.

The door through which William had entered the pantry opened from the dining-room. It stood wide open now, and Inspector Boyce could see the heavy figure of the butler fallen in a heap beside the table. That he was dead was past all question. That it was suicide seemed likely enough. And if it was suicide, then perhaps they need not look any farther for the murderer of Sir Francis Colesborough.

The Inspector tried the second door, and found it locked. Then he went over to the telephone and rang up the police station.

CHAPTER
TWENTY-NINE

"Not suicide?" said Colonel Anstruther.

"Well, I shouldn't say so. It's not impossible, you know." Dr Hammond's voice was brisk. "I'm not going to say it's impossible, but he was shot through the left temple, and he wasn't a left-handed man. Work it out for yourselves. I don't say it's impossible that a man who's going to commit suicide should take the pistol in his left hand and shoot himself through his left temple, but I don't believe it's ever happened. I mean, why should he? The thing's absurd. Besides —"

"There's this, sir," said Inspector Boyce. He leaned across the writing-table at which Colonel Anstruther was sitting and laid upon the blotting-pad a green silk handkerchief checked with brown.

"Bless my soul — what's that?"

"Handkerchief the missing letters were tied up in, sir. Lady Colesborough has identified it. You can see where the edge of the letters has marked it, and where the corners have been knotted."

"Well?" said Colonel Anstruther, staring.

"Where are the letters, sir? That's the point."

"He burnt 'em. How's that, Brook?"

Mr Brook shook his head.

"There was only a very small fire, sir," said the Inspector — "pretty well dead. Sturrock had been out for the afternoon, you know. If he'd tried to burn the letters, there'd have been some ash about. There wasn't any. And if he was Mr Zero and he'd got back letters incriminating him by murdering Sir Francis, he'd have destroyed them right away, and destroyed the handkerchief too."

"How do you know he didn't destroy 'em at once?"

"Marks on the handkerchief," said Inspector Boyce. "Very soft silk, sir. See — there's the shape of the envelopes quite plain, but the crease wouldn't last tumbling about in his pocket like he had it — not in that soft silk, not above an hour or so."

"What do you say to that, Brook?"

The four men were alone in the study. Mr Patterson, whose firm would as soon have touched divorce as murder, had gone back to town outraged in every susceptibility. Mr Montagu Lushington had not gone yet. He was, at the moment, in the drawing-room with his two secretaries.

"What do you say to that, Brook?"

Mr Brook nodded slightly.

"The Inspector is quite right, Colonel Anstruther. That handkerchief would only keep the shape of the letters for a very short time. If they hadn't been tied up in it for a good many hours, it wouldn't have kept it at all. I don't think it was suicide. Sturrock was the first on the scene of Sir Francis Colesborough's murder after Mr Somers and Miss Hardwicke ran up to the house. Lady Colesborough has said all along that she

211

didn't know what happened to the letters. Either she dropped them on her side of the hedge, or Mr Zero dropped them on his side. The brown and green silk covering would make the packet very inconspicuous. By some accident Sturrock found them. I think it is quite impossible that he should have been Zero, but I think the letters told him who Zero was. I think he tried to make use of this knowledge, and I think it brought him to his death. I think Mr Zero is a very dangerous man to blackmail."

Colonel Anstruther said, "Bless my soul!" in an extremely startled voice. Then he rallied. "Sounds like a lot of guesswork to me," he growled. "What about the pistol — what about fingerprints? They'll show who handled it."

"Only Sturrock's fingerprints on it, sir," said Inspector Boyce. "But of course anyone who was out to make it look like suicide wouldn't go leaving fingerprints of his own. Mr Brook is quite right, sir — Mr Zero is a dangerous one. And I don't think we've got to look very far for him either. It's getting enough evidence for a jury that's the trouble."

Colonel Anstruther looked up at him frowning.

"There's no doubt about the pistol being the missing one of Sir Francis Colesborough's pair?"

"Absolutely no doubt at all, sir. And who had the best opportunity of taking it? Why, he'd half an hour to do what he liked before we got here — hadn't he?"

Dr Hammond had been listening with brisk attention, turning his head from one speaker to another with rather the air of a terrier who is watching several ratholes at once. Very bright eyes and a head of tousled grey hair assisted the likeness. He burst now into speech.

"You mean Mr Somers?"

Colonel Anstruther pushed back his chair with a jerk.

"Oh, have him in — have him in! It's a crazy case, if you ask me."

The Inspector made for the door, but stopped with his hand on it. Mr Brook was speaking.

"Perhaps we had better see Mr Brewster first. Mr Lushington will be wanting to get back to town. If you have no objections, Colonel Anstruther —"

Colonel Anstruther had no objection, and presently Mr Brewster came in.

Before the door was shut Dr Hammond was up and taking his leave.

"I'd like to stay, but I've got to go. Twins at Railing, and a broken leg out at Oldmeadow. And it's Sunday evening. What a life!"

When he was gone Colonel Anstruther turned to Mr Brewster.

"Sit down, won't you? We won't keep you long, but we think you may be able to help us."

"Anything I can do." Mr Brewster registered an earnest desire to be helpful.

"Naturally. I believe you and Mr Somers left the drawing-room together after tea."

"Oh, yes, Colonel Anstruther, we did."

"Did you happen to notice the time?"

"Oh, yes — I glanced at my watch. It was twenty minutes past five. I thought Mr Lushington —"

"Yes, yes!" Colonel Anstruther's tone was testy. "Can you tell us what happened after you left the room?"

Mr Brewster assumed an intent expression.

"Yes, I can, Colonel Anstruther. And I assure you that I shall take great pains to be accurate. We came out of the drawing-room together — that is, Mr Somers and I came out of the drawing-room — and when we had got about half way across the hall — I think it was just about half way, but it may not have been quite as much — the butler came towards us from the direction, or what I now understand to be the direction, in which the domestic offices are situated."

"What? You saw Sturrock after you left the drawing-room?"

"If that is his name. We saw the unfortunate man who is the subject of the present enquiry."

"Bless my soul!" said Colonel Anstruther. "Make a note of that, Boyce. Well, that narrows down the time considerably. You saw Sturrock alive at twenty past five, and William found him dead at five-and-twenty to six. Well, go on, sir. What was he doing?"

"He approached us," said Mr Brewster, speaking in his precise way, "and he informed Mr Somers that he was wanted on the telephone."

"*What?*"

"I will endeavour to give you his exact words. To the best of my recollection he said, speaking to Mr Somers, 'There's a London call for you, sir. Perhaps you wouldn't mind taking it in my pantry as the gentlemen are using the study.'"

"Go on," said Mr Brook. "What happened after that?"

The Inspector wrote at Sir Francis Colesborough's table. Mr Brewster cast an interested glance at him and continued his narrative.

"Mr Somers disappeared in the direction from which the butler had come. I then enquired where it would be convenient for me to wait until Mr Lushington had finished his conversation with Mr Brook, and the butler indicated a room he called the Parlour. It is reached by a passage on the opposite side of the hall behind the drawing-room."

"Yes, yes!" Colonel Anstruther was impatient. "Did Sturrock accompany you along this passage?"

"No — he merely indicated the room."

"You went there?"

"I did."

"And remained there?"

"I remained there until about a quarter to six, when I thought I had really better make sure that Mr Lushington was still engaged. I found the house in a turmoil, and was informed that the butler had shot himself."

"That," said Mr Brook, "is by no means certain."

"Indeed?" Mr Brewster expressed a mild surprise.

"The Parlour is some way off," said Colonel Anstruther. "Did you see anyone at all during the time you were there?"

"No."

"Or hear anything? You didn't hear the shot?"

"Oh, no, sir. I think it would have been quite impossible to do so, having regard to the distance —"

"Yes, yes! Well, I think that's all — eh, Mr Brook? I don't think we need keep you any longer, Mr Brewster, and I don't think we need detain Mr Lushington if he wants to be off. Boyce, will you ask Somers to come here?"

CHAPTER
THIRTY

Algy Somers came into the room somewhat heartened by the fact that Monty had just clapped him on the shoulder and bidden him brace up. There had been real warmth in voice and manner. And he had always thought Monty rather a cold fish. It only showed that you never could tell.

He took the chair which Mr Brewster had vacated, but experienced none of his desire to be helpful. He felt an extraordinary distaste for the whole thing, an extraordinary mental fatigue. Through this fatigue came the conviction that the hostility he had encountered before had sensibly increased, and that they were all watching him as if they expected something to happen. He didn't know what.

Colonel Anstruther led off with the same question as before.

"You left the drawing-room with Mr Brewster. Did you notice the time?"

"Brewster did," said Algy. "He said it was twenty past five."

"Mr Brook corroborates that. He went in as you came out, and he looked at the clock in the hall. Now,

Mr Somers, will you tell us just what happened after you left the room?"

"Yes," said Algy. "Sturrock came through the baize door beyond the dining-room and said I was wanted on the telephone. He said it was a trunk call and would I mind taking it in the pantry."

"Yes?" said Mr Brook.

"I went through and took off the receiver. There was no one on the line. I tried to get the exchange, but they seemed to be asleep. When I did get them they said they didn't know anything about a trunk call. I hung up and came back into the hall."

"One minute, Mr Somers — how long did this take?"

"I can't say — two minutes — three — it always seems a long time when you're trying to get the exchange."

"And you say you returned to the hall?"

"Yes, I came back into the hall."

"Meeting Sturrock on the way?"

"No, I didn't see him again."

"You're sure he didn't come back into the pantry while you were at the telephone?"

"Oh, quite sure."

"And he wasn't in the hall when you got back there?"

"Not a sign of him."

"What did you do next, Mr Somers?"

"I went upstairs," said Algy. Like a cold wind the thought went over him that no one had seen him go.

Mr Brook's voice echoed the thought, inverting it, putting it to him as a question.

"Did anyone see you go upstairs? Did you meet anyone?"

"Not a soul, I'm afraid."

"What did you do when you got up there?"

"I went to my room."

"Yes?"

"I stayed there until I heard a commotion in the house. Then I came down, and someone, one of the footmen, told me Sturrock had shot himself."

"How long were you in your room?" said Colonel Anstruther.

"I couldn't say exactly, sir — about ten minutes."

There was a pause. Then the Chief Constable said,

"Listen to me, Mr Somers. The theory that this man Sturrock committed suicide is not borne out by the medical evidence. It is a very convenient theory, but it won't hold water. Very disappointing for the person who shot him, but there it is. It is our business to find out who did shoot him. Now here are the facts. Sir Francis Colesborough owned a pair of pistols. He kept one of them in that drawer — second on the right, wasn't it, Boyce? — and there is no evidence as to where he kept the other. Sturrock thought he kept them both there. Pity we didn't press the point at the time, but it wasn't of any special importance then — now of course it is. Sir Francis was shot with one of the pair, and Sturrock with the other. Now, supposing the second pistol to have been in that drawer, who had access to it before the police arrived last night?"

"A good many people, I should say, sir."

"Yourself among them. You agree to that?"

"Oh, certainly."

Colonel Anstruther frowned in a judicial manner.

"You had access to the weapon?"

"Oh, no, sir — that is going too far. I, in common with the entire household, had access to a drawer in which you suppose the second pistol may have been. There is no proof that it was there. I certainly never set eyes on it myself."

Colonel Anstruther said, "Tcha! Since Sturrock was shot with this pistol, it is obvious that it was on the premises, and if it was on the premises, you had access to it."

Algy shook his head.

"I don't admit any of that," he said.

Colonel Anstruther's colour deepened.

"Perhaps you will allow me to continue. Sturrock was shot between twenty-one or twenty-two minutes past five, when you and Mr Brewster encountered him in the hall, and five-and-twenty to six, when William found him dead and gave the alarm. During that time Mr Brook was with the Home Secretary in the drawing-room. Mr Patterson, myself, and the Inspector were in here. Mr Brewster was in the Parlour, Lady Colesborough in her own room with Miss Hardwicke, who says she left her to go to her bedroom a little before the half hour, but she was not away more than a minute or two. The staff were all in the servants' hall with the exception of the cook and the second housemaid, who were out, and Sturrock, whom none of them had seen from the time he had taken tea into the drawing-room at five o'clock. The wireless was switched on and a programme of military band music was coming through. This would account for the fact that nobody heard the shot. The servants were all together till just after the half hour, when William tried the pantry door and found it locked. There is a passage between the servant's hall and the pantry, and the doors are some distance apart. As William could get no reply, he became alarmed and, going round by the dining room, found the butler dead on the pantry floor with the pistol close to his hand. Now, Mr Somers, who shot him? He didn't shoot himself, you know — Dr Hammond is quite clear about that. He was shot by Mr Zero whom he was blackmailing."

Mr Brook, watching closely, saw Algy Somers start. A man may start when he is surprised, or when he is alarmed. Mr Brook went on watching closely, and Colonel Anstruther went on talking.

"Blackmailing," he said in a tone which dared anyone to contradict him. "Does that surprise you?"

"Very much," said Algy.

Colonel Anstruther said, "Tcha!" and continued, "There is evidence to show that Sturrock had been in possession of the letters which Lady Colesborough was about to hand over to Mr Zero when Sir Francis interrupted them. She must have dropped them, and Sturrock must have picked them up — he had ample opportunity before the police arrived. Anyhow he had them. The handkerchief in which they were wrapped was found on him."

"And the letters?"

"Mr Zero's got them. He did murder for them, and he got away with them. But he hasn't got clear, Mr Somers, and I don't think he will."

"I hope he won't," said Algy in rather an odd tone. Absent-minded, almost as if he was thinking of something else, was what Mr Brook thought. Then his head came up with a jerk, and he said in quite a different voice and manner, "Colonel Anstruther, may I tell you something?"

The Inspector looked up quickly. Colonel Anstruther stared.

"If you've anything to say — any information to give —"

"Well, I have, sir. I don't know what you'll think of it, but it seems to me that it might be important."

"Tell us what it is, Mr Somers," said Mr Brook.

"It's this," said Algy. "I expect you know that I took my car out this afternoon." His eye had a challenging sparkle. "Well, just beyond the gate I passed Sturrock ploughing along in the mud in his store clothes, and I offered him a lift. He said Railing would suit him, and I didn't care where I went, so I dropped him there in the Market Square, and as I was driving off I saw him go into a pub called the Hand and Flower." He stopped and Colonel Anstruther said,

"Is that all?"

Algy looked at him seriously.

"It doesn't sound very much, sir, but when you said Sturrock had been blackmailing Mr Zero, this is what struck me — if he had the letters, he must have found them last night. I told you we met him on the lawn and sent him down to where Sir Francis was lying, with orders to stay there until the police arrived. If he had the letters, that's when he got them, and if he used them to blackmail Mr Zero, the letters must have told him who Mr Zero was."

"Quite so," said Mr Brook drily.

"Well then, he would have to get into touch with him. If he was shot because he was blackmailing Mr Zero, it was because he did get into touch with him. Well, how did he do it? Would he risk using the telephone here, or would he think Railing safer? Why did he go to Railing anyhow? He was back again in time to bring in tea, you know. He told me he would be catching a bus at something after four. Don't you think there must have been something special to take him in to Railing if he was only going to be there for a little over half an hour? Wouldn't it be worth while to find out what he was doing in the Hand and Flower, and, if possible, whether he put through any telephone call whilst he was there? Someone may have noticed him."

Inspector Boyce looked up.

"That's a good idea, sir. I could send Collins. He's smart."

Colonel Anstruther sanctioned the sending of Collins with a grunt and a jerk of the head.

Algy got up.

"I've told you all I know, sir. Is there anything else?"

If they were going to arrest him, it would be now. He wondered what they had found in Francis Colesborough's safe. He wondered whether his red herring was going to give him a respite. He wondered what Gay was doing. Everything seemed to hang in the balance. Then Colonel Anstruther said stiffly,

"Nothing more at present, thank you, Mr Somers."

CHAPTER
THIRTY-ONE

Mr Lushington decided not to go back to town. Mr Brewster was instructed to ring up Railing Place and say that Mr Lushington was returning there.

"And you too of course." Constance Wessex-Gardner's voice was arch.

Mr Brewster reflected that it was a mistake to be arch when nature had provided you with a sharp, bony profile and a long, thin neck. He pictured them, shuddered faintly, and replied with his usual politeness that Mrs Wessex-Gardner was indeed kind, and that he would be delighted.

"These politicians," said the lady — "always so terribly busy. My brother-in-law never has a moment, but I hope that you will have some time to spare for me."

Mr Brewster departed from the stricter ways of truth and said he hoped so too. After which he reported to his chief, and they presently drove away together.

Mr Lushington appeared to be in a communicative mood.

"Most extraordinary affair," he said.

"Most inexplicable," said Mr Brewster. He paused, hesitated, and coughed slightly. "Would it be indiscreet if I were to enquire whether anything of importance was discovered in the safe?"

Montagu Lushington frowned.

"Mass of stuff — mostly irrelevant, I should say. They haven't had time to go through it all yet, but from what Brook tells me there's not much doubt that Colesborough was a most complete wrong 'un — had been for years — brought up to it by his old ruffian of a father. It seems that the old man went off the deep end at being given a baronetage instead of the barony he had set his heart on. There's a packet of letters about it, all written to the son, saying he'd get his own back — score the Government off — score the country off. The man must have been insane. Francis Colesborough too for that matter. That's proved by his keeping the letters. Incredible, isn't it?"

"Most astonishing," said Mr Brewster in his prim voice.

"The old man's been dead fifteen years, but Colesborough kept the letters. It's astonishing how people do keep things. Colesborough kept some pretty compromising stuff. Brook showed me a scheme of sabotage which would have paralyzed production in every factory in the country. It was headed 'To be applied in case of Emergency A.' Nice stuff to find in the safe of a man who held big government contracts! It seems to me that Mr Zero deserves a public vote of thanks instead of the hanging he'll get when they catch him."

Mr Brewster coughed again.

"Is there nothing in the safe that would give a clue as to his identity?"

"They haven't come across anything yet," said Montagu Lushington. He gave a heavy sigh. "It's a bad business. I'm afraid they'll arrest Algy Somers."

Mr Brewster made a shocked sound.

"Oh, surely not, sir!"

"If I felt sure of that, or of anything else in this case, I should sleep better tonight."

The Home Secretary was driving his own car. He looked straight ahead along the dark road and saw no end to it.

"Did they find that paper in the safe, sir?" said Mr Brewster.

Montagu Lushington came back from a long way off. He had been thinking that they would probably arrest Algy tonight, and if not tonight then certainly tomorrow, unless something turned up to incriminate someone else. And if Algy were arrested, he intended to place his own resignation in the hands of the Prime Minister.

He said, "What paper?" and Mr Brewster explained.

"The one you missed at Wellings, sir. I thought it might have turned up. You said Lady Colesborough had confessed to taking it, and I thought —"

"You made a mistake then. I certainly did not tell you that Lady Colesborough had taken the paper."

"It must have been somebody else," said Mr Brewster in a distressed voice, "but I really can't think who. Somers perhaps. Yes, now I come to think of it, I believe it was Somers."

Montagu Lushington laughed impatiently.

"It doesn't matter in the least, nor does the paper — now. What mattered was the list of suspected agents which was attached to the memorandum. Once Colesborough and his organization had seen that list and knew which of their men had come under suspicion, they could warn them, change them, substitute others. That was what mattered. Once Zero or Colesborough had seen the paper, the cat was out of the bag. They wouldn't keep the paper — they wouldn't want it."

"Dear me — I'd no idea," said Mr Brewster.

"Nobody had," said Montagu Lushington drily. "The fewer people who knew the better. I was keeping the information under my hat until the raid was over."

"The raid?" Mr Brewster spoke in a tone of surprise.

"Oh, it didn't come off. It wasn't worth while. The birds would have flown."

Mr Brewster said, "Dear me!"

Whilst the Home Secretary was driving towards Railing, Inspector Boyce was receiving a report from the smart young constable whom he had sent to make enquiries at the Hand and Flower.

"Sturrock was quite well known there, sir — regular customer — used to drop in in his off time and play a game of billiards. But he didn't play this afternoon. He didn't stay very long."

"What did he do?"

Collins looked chagrined.

"Well, I don't know that he did anything, sir."

"Did he use the telephone?"

"Well, sir, they don't know, and that's the truth of it. He might have done, but there's no one can say for sure. The telephone-box isn't in the hall any longer. They used to have it there, but they've moved it to a sort of recess outside the smoke-room. Mr Rudge, the proprietor, says he met Sturrock coming along the passage to the smoke-room. They had a bit of a chat — Mr Rudge says about nothing in particular, but if the truth was known, I expect it was Sir Francis Colesborough's murder they were talking about, Mr Rudge not being one to miss a chance like that, if you don't mind my saying so, nor I shouldn't be surprised if they'd stood there for the best part of half an hour. Mr Rudge doesn't say that. All he says is they had a bit of a chat, and Sturrock went into the smoke-room to have a look at the papers. And that's all I got, sir.

"What about the exchange?"

"There were half a dozen calls put through from the hotel in the course of the afternoon. I spoke to the young lady on duty, and that's all she could tell me. She doesn't remember any of the numbers that were asked for — said she'd have a nervous breakdown if she was to start trying to remember all the calls she put through in a day. A bit off-hand, if you know what I mean." Collins frowned. Off-hand and worse, that's what she'd been. One of the kind that wants taking down a peg or two. He wouldn't mind having a shot at it himself. Bluest eyes he'd ever seen.

"Well, that doesn't get us any farther," said Inspector Boyce.

CHAPTER
THIRTY-TWO

The Chief Constable had departed. Mr Brook had departed. The contents of the safe had been removed. Sturrock's body had been removed. Inspector Boyce had retired from the scene. To all outward appearance it might have been any Sunday evening at Cole Lester with the butler off duty and William taking his place a thought unhandily.

"Actually," as Algy said to Gay — "actually, my dear, the eye of the police is very much upon us. There's a young-fellow-my-lad hanging round the place to see that I don't take the Bentley out and forget to bring it back, and there's a smart police pup in the lane with a motor-bike all ready to follow me if I do. And William is going around like a cat on hot bricks looking at me out of the tail of his eye. I think he's thrilled at the idea of being at such close quarters with a murderer, but every now and then he gets an agonized feeling that I may have an urge to add him to the bag."

Gay stamped her foot and said, "I wish you wouldn't!"

She had come down to look for Algy and had come upon him in the study.

Algy laughed and she flashed into anger.

"I can't think why we go on talking about it, and I can't think why we're in this horrible room! It simply reeks of policemen!"

Algy really laughed this time. The other had been a pretense.

"What do policemen reek of?" he enquired from the depths of the largest chair.

"Red tape and sealing-wax!" snapped Gay.

Algy looked at her between half-closed lids. The room, purged of the police force, was pleasant enough. The Inspector had well and truly tended the fire, which now glowed like a sunset and diffused a most comforting warmth. There was a pleasant light from a tall lamp behind the chair. It fell on Gay, on the bright colour which anger had brought to her cheeks, on the shadows under her eyes. He thought she had been crying. He thought perhaps her eyelashes were still wet. He thought that perhaps he would never see her again. And he had an overwhelming desire to bid this moment stay, to halt it here, between the past and the future, between today and tomorrow, between the moment that had slipped from them and the moment that might never be for them at all. His heart said, "Stay," and it took him all he knew to keep his tongue still upon the word. He thought, "I love her," and thought how strange it was to feel this deep stab of triumph and pain. He thought, "She loves me too," and the triumph rushed up in him like a singing flame and consumed the pain. But he hadn't moved. The big chair held a lazy, lounging young man looking with half-closed eyes at an angry, pretty girl.

The sight exasperated Gay, who was only too eager to be exasperated. If she could be really furious with Algy, everything wouldn't hurt so much. It was when she was sorry for him, when she wanted to put her arms round him and keep him safe, that the pain at her heart became almost unendurable. "Only you've got to endure it — you've got to — you've *got* to." And if they sent Algy to prison, she would have to bear it for years, and years, and years. She didn't get any farther than Algy being sent to prison. She *wouldn't* get any farther than that. There are things you mustn't look at even for a moment, because they are too dreadful to be borne. Other people had to bear them, but not you. Things like that couldn't possibly happen to you. Don't look. Shut your eyes. Push them away, and bang, and bolt, and bar the door upon them. Anger is a great help when you are trying to bang that sort of door.

And then all at once such a little thing betrayed them both. Gay saw Algy looking at her. He didn't look lazy any more. His eyes were open and he was looking at her as if he loved her with all his heart, and as if he was saying goodbye — to love, to her, to everything. It was only for a moment, but that moment broke her anger and her pride, and very nearly broke her heart. She came over to the chair with a rush and went down on her knees by it, leaning to him across the arm, her hands holding it, her voice breaking on his name.

"Algy!"

232

It was no good. They had lost their balance, and when you have lost your balance you catch at anything or anyone. These two caught at one another, held desperately together across the arm of the chair, kissed desperately as if there were no other time but this in which to kiss, to love, to cling together — a time quick with anguish, quick with joy.

It passed, but it left them in a new country. They drew back, still holding hands, looking at one another and at this place to which they had come with stumbling, half-unwilling feet. Double pain for both, and a double load to carry, double foreboding, double fear, and a frowning barrier between them and the double joy which would have made it all worth while. Yet when Algy said, "I didn't mean to let you know," Gay knew just how unendurable that would have been. She said so in a rush of words,

"Horrible of you! I'd have died. I felt as if I was going to — when you said — they were going to arrest you."

"But, darling, you must have known that I did care."

"I couldn't — I didn't! How could I? You were being completely strong and silent. Oh, darling, wouldn't it be lovely if Sylvia had never been born, and if there weren't any police?"

Algy kissed her, and said he didn't follow.

"*Dull!*" said Gay. "If Sylvia hadn't been born she wouldn't have married Francis Colesborough, and if she hadn't, I shouldn't have asked you to lend me your car, and we shouldn't have come hurtling down here in the middle of the night and getting mixed up in Francis

233

being murdered. There wouldn't have *been* any murder, and even if there had been, it wouldn't have mattered if there hadn't been any police."

After which lucid explanations she put her head down on his shoulder and found it comforting.

CHAPTER
THIRTY-THREE

Mr Zero opened the door of his room and came out upon a dimly lighted corridor. The light was at the far end, so that if anyone had been watching they would probably not have seen him, and they certainly would not have caught the slightest sound. The pile of the carpet was deep, and Mr Zero's movements were extremely quiet and controlled. The hour being a quarter before three in the morning, there was no one watching. The house slept a deep, safe, comfortable sleep. No one waked, no one stirred, no one saw Mr Zero descend the stair and cross the dark hall below.

He came out of the hall into a room at the back of the house. There was no light there. He groped his way to the window and unlatched it. Setting down a small attaché case which he had been holding, he put both hands to the window and raised the sash. He picked up the attaché case, climbed out, and drew the window gently down again to about an inch from the sill. Then he took a torch from his pocket and found his way round the house and down a drive. Coming out upon the road, he increased his pace and walked rapidly away into the dark.

About twenty minutes later he came to the place he was bound for, a deep pond lying a little way off the road. The night was still. The water gleamed faintly under the open sky.

Mr Zero bent to his case, took something out of it, and straightened up. His arm swung, and the something went spinning through the air to fall with a splash in the deepest part of the pond.

Mr Zero shut his attaché case and retraced his steps toward the road. There was a gate to be climbed, and just as he was getting over it a car came roaring down the hill. With the gate on the outer side of a very sharp bend, the car seemed to be coming straight at him. He had time to jump down from the gate with his case in his hand, but the lights caught him before he could turn away or throw up an arm to screen his face. A murderous spasm of anger shook him. The car swung to the bend and was gone. The tail-light showed its red spark and disappeared. Someone who was out late and was in a hurry to get home, damn him.

But five minutes later Mr Zero was quite comfortable in his mind again. The fellow was probably a returning roisterer, and must anyhow have had enough to do to negotiate that extremely awkward bend at the really reckless pace he had been making. People had no business to drive like that, but in this instance there were mitigating circumstances. If he had been going as slowly as he should have been, his headlights would have given Mr Zero a more protracted publicity, and Mr Zero passionately desired privacy. For the rest of the return journey he had it.

In less than half an hour he was in bed again, and long before the clock struck four he was asleep. What was there to keep him awake? The letters that named him were burned and their frail ash scattered. The police had Francis Colesborough's pistols and they were welcome to them. The silencer was at the bottom of a most deep, convenient pond. Mr Zero slept in peace.

The car which had taken the bend with the ease and speed of long practice continued upon its way. Dr Hammond had been out all day and most of the night and he was in a hurry to get home. When he had put away his car and locked the garage door he went through into the house, walking on tiptoe, because he always hoped that Judith wouldn't wake. But while he was getting out of his coat she was half way down the stair in her blue dressing-gown, with her black hair flying, and one cheek scarlet where it had been pressed against the pillow.

"My poor child — I thought you were never coming. Soup in the dining-room — come along and have some at once."

Jim Hammond grinned.

"You're an officious woman, Ju. Why can't you stay quiet in your bed instead of flying up like a jack-in-the-box? Can't trust me to find my way to the dining-room, can you?"

She linked her arm in his and pulled him along.

"Why are you so late?"

"Because the Meaker baby was. Ten pound boy — hideous — healthy — and they're all as pleased as Punch. Ju, get off to bed!"

"I'd much rather talk to you while you have your sandwiches."

The dining-room was warm and bright, the sandwiches were good, and the soup was hot. Dr Hammond experienced the tired man's inclination to stay where he was and not bother about going to bed. When Judith drove him he snapped at her, yet presently he interrupted his undressing to wander into her room.

"Funny thing happened when I was coming home. You know Hangman's Corner? Well, I came up to it pretty fast —"

"And some day you'll get into trouble, my child," said Judith, sitting up in bed.

"Don't interrupt, woman! I'm an extremely careful driver. Where was I?"

"At Hangman's Corner. And I do wish they'd call it something else."

"They won't because of the pond. Well, I was coming down over the hill, and the headlights picked up a man who was getting over the gate. What do you suppose he was doing there at that hour of the night?"

"Going to Hangman's Pond or coming away from it, I should say. That gate doesn't lead anywhere else."

"He was coming away," said Dr Hammond — "getting back over the gate into the road — and he looked scared to blazes."

"I don't wonder. He probably thought you were going to run him down gate and all."

Dr Hammond yawned.

"Funny thing is I thought I'd seen his face before, only I can't think where."

He drifted out of the room, and made short work of getting into his pyjamas, returning to switch out the light and announce as he got into bed,

"If anyone else thinks of having twins, tell 'em to drown 'em. Night, Ju."

Yet twenty minutes later his head came up from the pillow with a jerk. Judith Hammond, wooing a dream in which the Meaker baby was hers, felt justly annoyed at being not only awakened but shaken.

"Ju, I know who that fellow was."

"What fellow?" said Judith, half cross and half forlorn. Perhaps she and Jim would never have a child. Perhaps —

Jim Hammond stopped shaking her to thump the bed-clothes triumphantly.

"The fellow I saw getting over the gate. What a damned extraordinary thing!"

CHAPTER
THIRTY-FOUR

But, darling, you can't marry him, so what's the good of saying you're engaged?"

"I'm *going* to marry him," said Gay with a fighting sparkle in her eyes.

She and Sylvia were in the Parlour, Sylvia in an easy chair, and Gay on her knees before a reluctant fire. She gave it a vicious poke and repeated firmly,

"I'm going to marry him."

Sylvia leaned forward.

"But, darling, how can you? I mean, you can't marry him if he shot Francis, because they'll hang him, won't they? Besides we *are* cousins — aren't we, and I don't think it would be at all nice."

Gay whisked round with her cheeks burning.

"He did *not* shoot Francis! And they won't — they *won't!* Sylly, how dare you?"

Sylvia's lovely eyes widened.

"I thought they did if you shot people. I thought that's what they were for."

"He *didn't* shoot Francis!"

Sylvia was surprised.

"But, darling, it would be such a good thing. I mean, everyone thinks he did, and it would clear it all up and

240

settle everything, and the police would go away and not worry us any more. I do hate that old man with the red face — don't you? They say he bullies his daughters most dreadfully. What I can't understand is why they don't arrest Algy and take him away, because if he didn't do it, they could always let him out again, and if he did — well, I really don't think it's quite nice saying good-morning, and talking about the weather, and asking him to pass the salt — not if he shot Francis — I mean, well, is it?"

Gay caught her by the wrists.

"Sylly, he did *not* shoot Francis! Will you get that into your head and keep it there! If it's the only idea you've got in the world, stick to it! Algy — didn't — shoot — your — husband. It's as simple as pie. Have you got it? Then hold on to it tight and don't let go. *Algy didn't shoot Francis.*"

"Then who did?" said Sylvia simply.

"I don't know, but Algy didn't. And when you say you don't like having him in the house, you seem to forget that he's done nothing but say hadn't he better go to an hotel. And Colonel Anstruther kept on saying no and practically insisting on his staying here. You don't suppose he *wants* to — you don't suppose either of us want to? But of course the police like it because it gives them only one house to watch instead of sleuthing you in one place, and me in another, and Algy somewhere else."

Sylvia said, "Oh, well —" and spread her hands to the small, uneasy flame which had responded to Gay's last vigorous poke. "Of course," she continued, "I don't want Algy to be hanged if he really didn't do it, even if it would save a lot of trouble. But I don't think I should be engaged to him — just in case, you know."

"I *am* engaged to him," said Gay, with smiling lips.

"I know, darling. That's just how I felt when Mummy wouldn't let me go out with Frank Rutherford any more. He wanted me to be engaged, you know, and if it hadn't been for Mummy I might have married him."

"Suppose you had, Sylly?"

"Darling, he might have gone on being a curate for years, and years, and years, and I don't know what they get, but Mummy said it wasn't enough. And I cried dreadfully, but when Francis asked me to marry him, wasn't I thankful! Because it *doesn't* look nice if you have to break off an engagement — I mean, Francis being so rich, people would have been sure to talk, wouldn't they?"

Gay looked at her with a sort of fascinated interest.

"Do you mean that you would have broken off your engagement to Frank Rutherford if you had been engaged to him when Francis asked you?"

Sylvia heaved a sigh.

"It was much nicer not having to do it — wasn't it?"

"You mean you would have broken it off?"

Sylvia put her handkerchief to her eyes.

"I don't think you're being at all *kind*," she said, and dropped a tear, but whether for Frank or for Francis was more than Gay could tell. It was only a moment, however, before she looked up with a dawning interest in her eyes. "You know, darling, I rather liked the other one. Couldn't you be engaged to him instead?"

242

Gay stared, sat back on her heels, and said as firmly as her surprise would allow,

"What other one?"

"The nice polite one," said Sylvia. "I'm sure he would if you encouraged him a little. I think he's rather shy, but so polite. I think he'd make a really good husband."

If Sir Francis had been dead a little longer, Gay might have retorted, "Then marry him yourself." She decided regretfully that it wouldn't be decent. She said in an exasperated voice,

"I suppose you know what you're talking about, Sylly — I don't."

"That nice polite Mr Brewster. I really was sorry I didn't see him yesterday when he was here. He'd have been so nice and ordinary after that horrid Colonel Anstruther and all those policemen and people. I think it *would* be much better for you to be engaged to him."

Gay burst out laughing. She really couldn't help it.

"It's all very well to laugh," said Sylvia in a protesting voice, "but I do think it would be nice to have a safe, ordinary sort of person like Mr Brewster coming into the family. I mean, I really do think we want someone like that for a change. It isn't as if we'd been brought up to have criminals in the family, and now they all say Francis was, and you say *yourself* that Algy is going to be arrested. And what do you think Colonel Anstruther and Mr Brook said to me this morning? Why, they actually said they could send *me* to prison for taking that stupid envelope."

Gay had stopped laughing.

"I suppose they could," she said soberly.

"It's all right — they're not going to," said Sylvia in a reassuring tone. "They said they'd had a conference or something at headquarters, and they weren't going to, because they think it was Francis who made me, and Mr Brook said he didn't think I realized what I was doing, and there's some law about its being your husband's fault if he tells you to do something like that, so they're not going to arrest me. I think Mr Brook likes me a little, because I began to cry, and he said not to quite nicely. But Colonel Anstruther only glared and said, 'Tcha!'"

Gay felt a good deal of relief. She thought the law a very convenient one for Sylvia. She said,

"Why do they think it was Francis who made you take the paper? He couldn't have talked to you on the telephone without you knowing his voice."

"Oh, it wasn't Francis who talked to me on the telephone. I told them it wasn't, and they said they never thought it was. But they think Francis told him to do it — Mr Zero, you know — and told him what to say and all that."

"But why should he, Sylly? Why should Francis make you do a thing like that?"

Sylvia wrinkled her smooth white brow.

"He was very jealous about me," she said in a doubtful voice. "He thought a lot about being older than me, and he used to say things like, 'I'll never let you go. I'll find a way to keep you, my dear.' And once he said, 'I've thought of a way to put a chain round your neck, my sweet.' That was just before it all began

244

to happen, and when I asked him what he meant he said a very horrid thing. He said, 'You'll stay because you'll be afraid to go.'"

Gay said, "You think he made you take the paper so as to have a hold over you?"

Sylvia nodded.

"Of course, he wanted the paper too. And he needn't have been jealous — he ought to have known that. I mean, I'm not that sort — am I, darling? No one in our family ever has been — we just *don't*. And Mummy would have had a fit." Horror widened Sylvia's eyes. "Oh, *darling*, isn't it a good thing they're not going to arrest me? What *would* Mummy have said?"

CHAPTER
THIRTY-FIVE

Mr Brewster was turning things over in his mind. Like Gay Hardwicke, he felt considerably relieved to learn that there was no intention of putting the law in motion against Lady Colesborough. He had been too discreet to ask any direct question, but it had transpired that the lovely Sylvia would grace the witness box and not the dock. It should be a very interesting trial. The trouble was that until the dock could be, so to speak, filled, no trial would take place. Mr Brewster considered that Algy Somers would be very suitably cast for the part of prisoner at the bar. He had always disliked Algy a good deal, and although concealing this and some other emotions under a precise and formal manner, he now permitted himself to hope.

The matter which exercised him most was the exact line of conduct which it would be correct for him to pursue with regard to the widowed Lady Colesborough. The situation was a very delicate one. She was a newly made widow, and as such to be treated with all possible respect. He, as one of Mr Lushington's secretaries, must demean himself with the utmost possible tact and discretion. Yet it was in these very circumstances that an indelible impression might be made upon the feelings of a beautiful young woman who had been so suddenly and strangely bereaved. Now was the moment for delicate sympathy and loyal friendship, now was the moment to plant what might later burgeon and bear fruit. Francis Colesborough's widow was lovely, rich, and for the moment, friendless. Mr Brewster thought deeply on the possibility of stepping forward in a true spirit of chivalry to support and comfort the mourner. On the other hand he would have to be very careful, because it was now certain to come out that Lady Colesborough had compromised herself by abstracting papers from the Home Secretary's despatch-case. There might be no prosecution, but she would remain compromised, he could not afford to associate with persons whose probity was not above suspicion. It was all very delicate and required the most careful handling.

Mr Brewster looked at his watch and found the time to be half past three. He thought he would take a walk. Fresh air and exercise would assist his mental processes. A strong inclination to walk in the direction of Cole Lester presented itself. He was engaged in a prudent resistance, when the telephone bell rang and a voice demanded Mr Lushington. He recognized the voice as that of Mr Brook and made a note of the fact that the tone suggested urgency.

When staying at Railing Place, Mr Lushington was accommodated with a sitting-room which opened out of his bedroom. Both rooms were provided with telephone extensions. Mr Brewster informed his chief that he was wanted on the line and withdrew. But at the same moment that Mr Lushington was saying, "Hullo!"

his secretary was opening the bedroom door and very carefully closing it again. It was essential that he should discover what had brought that urgent tone into Mr Brook's voice. He crossed silently to the bedside instrument, lifted the receiver, and listened in. He had lost nothing except the preliminary "Hullo!" for he could hear the Home Secretary saying, "What is it, Brook?" And then Mr Brook, still with that subdued urgency, "Well, sir, I thought I had better tell you. There's something come to light among those papers we took out of the safe."

"Yes, Brook?" Montagu Lushington's tone was quiet.

"Well, sir, I'm afraid it's conclusive."

"Will you tell me what has been found?"

"A scrap of paper with a couple of lines of cipher on it — just a bit that had been torn off and had got caught up in a pile of bills. That's why it wasn't noticed before." Mr Brook's voice dropped a shade. "I've just had it decoded. It runs: 'To have one of Lushington's secretaries in our pay is worth all he asks — and more.' I'm sorry, sir, but I'm afraid it is quite conclusive. The Chief Constable is having Mr Somers arrested at once."

"I see," said Montagu Lushington in a tired voice. What he saw was family disgrace, public scandal, and the end of his own career.

Mr Brewster slipped quietly out of the bedroom, and downstairs and out of the house. Whatever prudence counselled, he was going to walk over to Cole Lester. It would be worth some risk to see Algy Somers arrested.

He took a short cut across the fields which would reduce the distance from five miles to three. The path presently skirted a deserted quarry and came by way of a rough cart track out upon the high road again.

CHAPTER
THIRTY-SIX

Algy Somers looked up from the letter he was trying to write and said, "Come in." The knock which he thought he had heard was so weak and hesitating that it might have been any chance sound. He was therefore faintly surprised when the door opened and displayed William in a condition of acute embarrassment.

"Yes?" said Algy. "What is it?"

William stood and twisted the handle. It went sharply through Algy's mind that the police had come to arrest him, and that William knew it. He managed a smile, and said,

"Out with it, William. What is it?"

William came a hesitating step into the room, let go of the handle, fumbled for it again, and reverting to a less polished standard than that set up by the late Mr Sturrock, reached with a nervous foot and kicked the door to behind him.

"If you please, sir —" he said, and stuck.

"Well, William?" said Algy.

William dragged a handkerchief from his cuff and wiped a clammy brow.

"If I might have a word with you, sir —"

Relief rushed in on Algy. So it wasn't his arrest — not yet. He said cheerfully.

"As many as you like. What's up, man? Why are you dithering?"

"I don't rightly know how to begin, sir." But the handkerchief went back into his cuff and his brow remained fairly dry.

"Begin at the beginning. What's it all about anyway?"

William turned bright plum colour.

"I've got a young lady, sir —"

Algy very nearly said, "So have I," but it seemed well to keep William to the point if possible, so he substituted an encouraging, "That sounds all right."

"She works at the Hand and Flower at Railing," said William.

Algy sat up and began to take notice.

"The deuce she does! Well, that's very interesting. What about it?"

William's forehead began to glisten again.

"It don't seem as if I ought to hold my tongue."

"Then I shouldn't."

"Only my young lady she don't want to be drawn into it, if you take my meaning, sir.

Algy laughed a little grimly.

"I don't suppose any of us wanted to be drawn into it."

"No, sir. All very well on the pictures murders are, but close at hand there's something 'orrid about them to my way of thinking."

"Two minds with but a single thought," said Algy. "Now what about coming to the point — getting the stuff off the chest?"

William produced the handkerchief again.

"Sunday nights when I have my evening out I go over to Railing, but Sunday nights when I don't my young lady she comes over here, and I can slip out and we do a bit of walk up and down in the lane, and last night —"

"You slipped out?"

"Yes, sir. And Ellen she says to me — her name is Ellen Hawkins and she's got a married sister that keeps a toy-shop in Railing — very nice people they are, and Ellen she's at the Hand and Flower —"

"What did she say?"

"Well, she hadn't heard about Mr Sturrock being shot. She'd had the afternoon off from four o'clock, so she wasn't there when the police come, and she didn't know nothing about it, and she says, 'Oh, William,' she says, 'how 'orrid! I wouldn't ha' come over if I'd ha' known.' And 'It don't seem hardly right, and you'll have to take me home, for I won't go by myself and that's flat,' she says, so I done it."

"Is that all?" said Algy after a prolonged pause.

William shook his head.

"Oh, no, sir. We got talking while we were going along like, and Ellen she told me something, and I told her she didn't ought to keep it to herself."

Algy regarded William with admiration.

"Good man! What did she tell you?"

"We had quite a difference of opinion about it, sir, and I don't say there wasn't something in what she said."

"Well, what did she say?"

"Well, she put it this way, sir — if the police come and asked her, she's be bound to tell them, and if they didn't ask her, then it wasn't none of her business. 'And look what come to poor Mr Sturrock,' she says. 'You won't make me nor anyone else believe that he didn't know something,' she says, 'and that's why he was done in. And I wish I'd held my tongue and not told you anything,' she says."

"What did she tell you?" said Algy.

William turned an even brighter plum.

"If you'll excuse me, sir, there's talk about the police thinking you done it. And I said to Ellen, 'You wouldn't let them go and arrest Mr Somers and all for the want of a word.' And that's where we had our difference of opinion, because Ellen she said she would — but of course she don't know you, sir."

"And you've known me how long? About a day and a half."

"It don't take as long as that to know what a gentleman's like," said William. "No one's going to make me believe you shot Mr Sturrock nor Sir Francis neither. Now the other —"

"That's very nice of you and all. And now suppose you tell me what Ellen told you."

"Well, sir, it was this way. Ellen's second housemaid at the Hand and Flower, and she hasn't any business in the smoke-room on a Sunday afternoon, so I wouldn't like to be getting her into trouble."

"You won't," said Algy. "Get on."

"Well, sir, it was her afternoon off like I told you, and she was all dressed to go out, and the smoke-room being empty, she slipped in to have a look at one of the papers there — something about the pattern of a dress she seen the picture of and was wanting to copy and she wasn't sure she'd got it right. Well, then she got a fright. She heard voices in the passage, and one of them was Mr Rudge, the proprietor. She didn't want him to find her there, so she stepped behind the curtain, which was a right-down silly thing to do, because it made her look as if she was doing something wrong. She took a look through the curtain, and the talking had stopped, and then she got another fright, because Mr Sturrock come into the room. He walked over to the table and stood looking down at the papers that was on it, and Ellen thought whatever should she do if he was going to stay. But he didn't. He went back to the door and looked along the passage, and after a minute he went out and Ellen she come out from behind the curtain, but when she got to the door, there was Mr Sturrock in the telephone-box right opposite, and she dursn't pass him, so she stayed where she was, and that's how it come that she heard what he was saying."

"Those boxes are supposed to be sound-proof, aren't they?"

"This one isn't, sir, because the door doesn't fit. There's a radiator quite near, and the wood's shrunk, so it won't stay shut, not all the way down. And Ellen

254

says she heard Mr Sturrock say, 'Is that you?' and she says she heard him name a name."

"What name?"

"And she heard him say, 'I've got to see you,' and then something about some letters and it's being worth his while. She says she didn't pay any particular attention because of watching her opportunity to slip out, but she does remember Mr Sturrock saying, 'It'll have to be in the house. I won't come out to meet you, and you know why. You bring the money, and I'll have the letters ready for you.' And then she got her chance because he turned clean away from her, and she ran for it."

"You said she heard a name."

William lost some of his ruddy colour.

"Mr Sturrock was shot, sir. I'd like to be sure about Ellen not coming to any harm."

"She can have police protection. She'll have to speak — she'll have to say what she knows. Come on, man, give me the name!"

William gulped.

"Ellen she heard Mr Sturrock say, 'Is that you?' and she heard him name a name, and she says it was Rooster."

Algy sat quite stiff for about a minute. Then he said, "What?" very softly, and William said,

"Rooster, sir."

There was another silence. Then Algy got up. His mind felt stiff and his tongue felt stiff, but he managed to say,

"Thank you very much, William."

He went out of the room and downstairs to the study, where he rang up Railing Place and asked if he could speak to Mr Montagu Lushington. He thought it would add an ironic touch to the situation if Brewster were presently to enquire whether he could take a message. Instead, Monty's voice, rather stiff and chilly:

"What is it?"

"Algy Somers speaking, sir. I want to come over and see you — at once, if I may."

"I hardly think that would be advisable." The voice had lost its last vestige of human warmth.

Very difficult to persist, but Algy persisted.

"Look here, sir, I've just heard something which I think is tremendously important. I think you ought to know what it is before I give it to the police. I can't tell you about it on the telephone. May I come over? It's — it's really important."

"I think it is inadvisable," said Montagu Lushington. After a moment's pause he added, "I think you might find it difficult to get here." The line went dead.

Algy hung up at his end, and thought, "That means I'm to be arrested . . . Monty wants to keep out of the mess . . . I don't blame him . . . It mightn't mean anything more than my not being allowed to leave Cole Lester . . ."

He looked at his watch. Twenty-three minutes to four. It would take him the best part of an hour to reach Railing Place. But something had been said about a short cut. He couldn't remember who had said it, but something had been said.

256

He sought out William, and decided that the short cut ought to be quite easy to follow. Of course, if he dared take his car — but he didn't dare. They might let him go out on foot, but he felt tolerably certain that any attempt to take the Bentley would land him out of the frying-pan and into the fire.

He strolled down the drive and into the lane. A very young policeman looked at him uncertainly and let him pass.

Algy continued to stroll until he was out of sight, when he began to walk as fast as he could. William had given him two short cuts, and the first one took off no more than a quarter of a mile away, for which he felt duly grateful. He climbed a stile, cut across a couple of fields, and got back to the road again by way of a little wood. At about ten minutes past four he was approaching the second short cut, which led past a disused quarry and a number of fields to Railing Place.

CHAPTER
THIRTY-SEVEN

Mr Brewster had arrived at this point a few minutes before. He was not nearly so fast a walker as Algy Somers and he had not hurried himself. His thoughts were pleasant and he savoured them with enjoyment. He looked idly at the quarry as he skirted it. It was deep, and must have been long in disuse, for there were saplings growing here and there in the clefts, and a great tangle of blackberry bushes sprawled, climbed, and clung about its sides.

He went forward with the track and came out upon the road. There was a car coming from the direction of Railing. Dr Hammond, at the wheel, saw a man emerge from the old cart track and, recognizing Mr Brewster, trod hard on his brakes and came sliding up beside him. Mr Brewster turned, and the car stopped.

Dr Hammond opened the door, leaned out of it, and said,

"Hullo! Your name's Brewster, isn't it?"

Mr Brewster in his primmest manner admitted it.

Dr Hammond leaned a little farther out, his prematurely grey hair sticking up in tufts, his eyes more than ever like those of a terrier — a terrier who sees a rat. The bright spark in them alarmed Mr Brewster.

258

This man was the police surgeon. He slid a nervous hand into his pocket.

Dr Hammond said in his sharp, barking voice,

"Met you at Cole Lester yesterday, didn't I?"

"I believe so — if you can call it meeting."

"You came in, and I went out. That's how it was, wasn't it? But I never forget a face."

"A very useful faculty," said Mr Brewster with his hand in his pocket.

"Sometimes." Jim Hammond grinned. "Can I give you a lift, Mr Brewster?"

"No thanks, I have come out for some exercise."

"Glutton for exercise, aren't you? Do you often take it at three in the morning?"

"I really don't —" Mr Brewster's hand was coming out of his pocket.

"I saw you getting over the gate at Hangman's Corner last night. My headlights picked you up. I think the pond up there is about due for a clean out. Hangman's Pond they call it. Nasty name. Nasty insanitary pond. I'm going to recommend its being cleaned out, Mr Brewster —"

The name broke off a little short, because Mr Brewster's hand had come up level with Dr Hammond's eyes and it held a small automatic pistol.

"Put your hands up and keep them up!" said Mr Brewster sharply. "Sit right back — I'm going to shut the door!" He did so, opened the rear door with his left hand, and got in.

Dr Hammond felt the muzzle of the pistol cold against the back of his neck and cursed aloud.

"Be quiet!" said Mr Brewster. "You can put your hands down now. I want you to start the car and drive down that field track — the one I came out of just now. You'll have to reverse."

With his hands on the wheel and the engine purring, Dr Hammond said in a tone of concentrated fury,

"What damn fool game is this?"

"Drive along that track!" commanded Mr Brewster.

Dr Hammond gritted his teeth and did as he was told. What a fool he had been. The fellow meant to kill him. A double murderer already, he couldn't afford to let him go. Play for time — that was the only thing. Stave it off and watch for the odd, improbable chance. He thought about Judith his wife and his heart was full of bitter rage.

"Stop here!" said Mr Brewster in that new sharp voice.

They were round a bend and out of sight of the road. The car stopped, and in a flash the pistol which had been pressed against the back of Dr Hammond's neck was levelled at his temple. It was still in Mr Brewster's hand, but Mr Brewster was now standing outside the car looking in upon the driver's seat. Jim Hammond's moment had come and gone. He ought to have ducked and jumped for it the moment the pistol moved, but the whole thing had been so unbelievably quick. He had had his chance and lost it.

"Hands up!" said Brewster. "And get out!" He opened the door and stood back enough to be out of reach. I'm a dead shot, Hammond, so no tricks. I'd rather shoot you than not, because it would be safer for me, but I'll give you a chance if you do what you're told. Walk along the track in front of me and don't let your hands down!"

Jim Hammond thought, "He can't let me go. Why doesn't he shoot and get it over?" And the answer, "He'll drop me at the edge of the quarry — save him the trouble of dragging me there. No, not me, the body — Jim Hammond's body."

The cart track ran within twenty yards of the quarry's edge. When they reached this point Mr Brewster gave another order.

"Turn right! Leave the track and go towards the quarry!"

It was rough, broken ground. Dr Hammond had many thoughts. None of them promised very much. He thought of a sudden dodging swerve and a quick tackle. But he had to turn — he had to turn — and the pistol was no more than a yard away. The quarry's edge was no more than a yard away.

CHAPTER
THIRTY-EIGHT

Algy turned off the road into the field track. This looked as if it was the right place, but he would soon know because of the quarry. William had made rather a point of the quarry, but you couldn't see it from the road. The track was muddy, and a car had been over it recently. How any springs could be expected to stand up to these ruts was beyond him.

In a minute or two he came in sight of the car. The track swung to the right about a thicket of holly, yew, and leafless oak, and there, nicely tucked away, was the car, a V.8 Ford, and beyond it the quarry. He walked on, and a sound came to him, the sound of Brewster's voice, and yet not Brewster's. He heard the voice before he heard any words, and before he saw either of the two men upon the quarry's edge. The car hid them. As he came on, the sound became words, the most unbelievable words.

"I'm going to shoot you. Take your hands down and I shoot at once. Keep them up and you have another minute or two to live. You despise me, don't you? You thought I should cringe and ask you to hold your tongue. You made a great mistake. You made the same mistake that Francis Colesborough made. He thought he could use me, threaten me. Well, he had to pay for that. Sturrock paid the same price. He actually thought he could blackmail me, poor fool. Was that your game too, Dr Hammond?"

Algy had reached the car. He heard Dr Hammond snap out, "No, it wasn't!" and he heard Brewster laugh, which was a surprising thing in itself because he had never heard Brewster laugh before. The sound was a strange and horrifying portent.

He looked cautiously round the car and saw Dr Hammond a yard from the quarry's lip, facing him with his hands above his head, and close to him Brewster with a pistol in his hand. They were about twenty yards away. If he were to shout, to run, what would happen? He thought that pistol would go off, and he thought Dr Hammond would be a dead man. Suppose he sounded the horn. Would it make Brewster turn his head for just the fraction of a second which would give the Doctor his chance? He thought the pistol would still go off and put an end to Jim Hammond's chances once and for all. The man who had shot Sturrock in his own pantry and got away with it must have a quite unshakable nerve.

As he thought these things, he was moving towards the quarry. That was the only real chance there was — to get nearer, to get near enough to startle the murderer out of his aim by rushing him. Even if he was heard, that might help. Brewster would be disturbed. He wouldn't know what the sound was — whether he had really heard it. He would be tempted to look round and have to fight his own fear of being taken from behind.

The rough tussocky grass deadened the sound of his feet. He had got to within half a dozen yards, when Mr Brewster's voice changed. He said, "I'm tired of you. Out you go!" and fired.

Algy's shout and the shot rang out almost together. Dr Hammond pitched forward into the quarry, and Mr Brewster whisked round with the pistol in his hand. Algy ran in, swerved, ducked, and got him round the knees. A shot went wide. They came down together.

Algy had the surprise of his life. Falling on Cyril Brewster was like falling on an eel — an eel that writhed, contorted itself, twisted, and was out of his grasp. As he rose on his knees, he saw that Brewster was up already, and that the muzzle of the pistol was only a yard away.

"If you move you're dead. Hands up!"

"I'm dead anyhow," said Algy. He put up his hands. Cyril Brewster nodded.

"Quite right. But just a word first. I've disliked a great many people in my life, but I've hated you. Now I'm going to pay off my score."

"But, good heavens, why? I mean, why should you hate me? I've never —"

"Haven't you?" said Mr Brewster. "Think again! My people had to skimp and save to give me a good education. I took scholarships or they couldn't have done it. You were probably never more than half way up your form. You didn't have to work. You had time for games — I hadn't. And so you despise me."

"Brewster, you're mad."

264

"I assure you that I am not. I am your superior in every possible way, but you despise me because — you have money, and I haven't — you are an athlete, and I'm not — you have been to a famous school, and I haven't. Well, now I've got you on your knees to me."

At this point Algy got to his feet. He was certainly for it. He preferred to be shot standing up.

Mr Brewster did not shoot yet. He said sharply,

"Keep your hands up! I want to tell you what has happened and what is going to happen. You have just shot Dr Hammond because he had discovered that you were Mr Zero. You are about to commit suicide. You will be found with the pistol in your hand."

"And a full confession in my left boot?" said Algy pleasantly.

Something was happening. He was facing the quarry and Mr Brewster had his back to it. Behind that back something was happening. A hand had come over the lip of the quarry, a very scratched, dirty hand. It felt for a hold and found it. The other hand appeared. Dr Hammond's head appeared. There was blood running down over his forehead. His hair stood bolt upright. He showed all his teeth in a vicious grin.

Algy said, "I still don't see why you hate me so much, you know. You've simply imagined all that about my despising you. Good lord, man, one doesn't go about despising people!"

Dr Hammond got a knee over the edge, flung himself forward, and plucked Mr Brewster's ankles from under him. A bullet went singing past Algy's cheek as he ran in. There were two of them now to grapple with that twisting eel, and the two of them had their work cut out.

"The pistol, man — get the pistol!" snapped Jim Hammond, who had been kicked in the face.

Algy got a whirling arm and a wrenching wrist. The pistol went off again. Cyril Brewster's teeth met in his thumb and with another twist he was free.

The police car came round the corner, bumping over the ruts and bumping off them across the rough ground between the track and the quarry. Inspector Boyce jumped out. Police Constable Collins and the tall young man who had looked doubtfully at Algy in the lane jumped out. They saw three men all running in a very surprising order, because Mr Brewster, the Home Secretary's secretary, had the lead. He also had a pistol in his hand. Mr Somers, whom they had come to arrest, was running him close, and hard upon his heels Dr Hammond, collarless and dishevelled, with a hand to his jaw.

Mr Brewster gained a little and, coming round the turn, looked across a quarter circle and saw the second car, the Inspector, and the two policemen. They saw him look down at the pistol in his hand, and they saw him turn and aim at Algy Somers. They heard the crack of the shot.

Perhaps Mr Brewster had been boasting when he claimed to be a dead shot, perhaps his wrenched wrist betrayed him. He missed handsomely and, with Algy closing in, turned the pistol on himself and did not miss. From the lip of the quarry he stepped back and went crashing down to the rock and the brambles below.

266

CHAPTER
THIRTY-NINE

If I hadn't the jaw-bone of an ox, he'd have broken it," said Dr Hammond wrathfully. "Boyce, you're blithering. Mr Somers hasn't murdered anybody. He's just escaped being murdered by the skin of his teeth, and so have I. Your Mr Zero, the man who murdered Sir Francis Colesborough and Sturrock and did his damnedest to shoot Mr Somers and myself, is at the bottom of the quarry, and you'd better send your men down to make sure he's dead. I'd send two of them if I were you, because if he isn't dead he'll be about as safe as a wounded tiger. I'm not going down and that I tell you flat. They can bring him up here to me. I've had some and I'm not going down again." He clutched rather suddenly at Algy and lowered himself on to the grass.

"You're not hurt, sir?" Boyce's tone was full of concern.

"Shook up," said Dr Hammond rather faintly. He shut his eyes and leaned forward with his head on his knees.

"Perhaps you'll tell us what's been happening, Mr Somers," said the Inspector. "We went after you to

Cole Lester, and when we found you weren't there, well, it was natural for us to draw certain conclusions."

"I suppose it was," said Algy. "But I was only walking over to Railing Place. I wanted to see Mr Lushington."

"That's what William told us. We had just got to the turn where the track comes in, when we heard the shooting and got a move on. Lucky we arrived when we did."

"Yes. He knew the game was up as soon as he saw you. As long as it was only the Doctor and me, he'd have gone on fighting. He meant it to look as if I'd shot Dr Hammond and then committed suicide."

Jim Hammond lifted his head for a moment and nodded.

"He'd got it all planned," he said. "I'm going to have a lump on my jaw like a turkey's egg."

"Will you tell us what happened, Mr Somers?" said the Inspector.

Algy was tying a handkerchief round his thumb.

"William told me about the short cuts. He told me something else too. His girl heard Sturrock ring Brewster up on Sunday afternoon — she's the housemaid at the Hand and Flower. That is what I was going to see Mr Lushington about. I thought he ought to know before anyone else did."

"I don't know that you were right about that, sir."

Algy lifted a hand and let it fall again.

"Well, that's what I thought. I came round that corner and saw Dr Hammond's car, and when I got clear of the car I saw Dr Hammond. He was standing on the edge of the quarry with his hands above his head and Brewster holding him up with a pistol. I tried to get there without being heard, but he suddenly loosed off his gun and the Doctor went over the edge. I thought he was done for. I don't know why he wasn't."

Dr Hammond's head came up again.

"I jumped," he said with a wry grin. "Brewster said, 'I'm tired of you. Out you go!' But I didn't wait for the word go — I beat the pistol. And those infernal brambles practically skinned me alive."

"Better alive than dead, sir," said Inspector Boyce. He looked at Algy with a dubious expression. "Well, sir, all this is a bit awkward for me. You see, what with one thing and another, the evidence had got pretty well piled up against you, and — well — it's a bit awkward, but I've got a warrant for your arrest."

Dr Hammond gave a groan.

"Boyce, you continue to blither, and I warn you that I am in no state to be blithered at. That's my professional opinion. Free, gratis, and for nothing. Here, give me a hand up — I don't want a crick in the neck as well as a sock on the jaw." He groaned again as he got to his feet. "Now, Boyce, get this into your head. The, I hope, late Mr Brewster murdered Sir Francis Colesborough and Sturrock, and did his best to murder Mr Somers and me. He boasted about Sir Francis and the butler — I heard him. Mr Somers saw him shoot at me, and I saw him shoot at Mr Somers. Now what's your damn fool warrant worth? Hang it all, man, you can't go arresting him now!"

Inspector Boyce coughed slightly.

"If you were feeling up to it, sir, what I would suggest would be for you and Mr Somers to go along with me to see the Chief Constable —"

"I don't feel up to it," said Dr Hammond bitterly. "I feel very ill. I require a strong stimulant, a nice hot bath, and a complete change of clothing. But I'm a martyr to duty."

A hail came up from the quarry. The Inspector went and looked over the edge.

"Found him?" he called out.

"Yes, sir."

"Dead?"

"Yes, sir."

"Well, that's going to save everyone a lot of trouble," said Dr Hammond.

CHAPTER
FORTY

Darling, I think it went off *too* marvellously," said Sylvia Colesborough. She shed her grey fur coat and leaned back in the sofa corner. "Algy darling, ring for tea, will you? I could drink cups, and cups, and cups. I didn't think anyone could ask so many questions as that Coroner did. But he was rather sweet too. Didn't you think it was rather sweet of him to say he quite understood how upset I must be feeling?"

Gay giggled — she couldn't help it. The giggle slid off into something like a sob. They had just come back from an inquest upon the two murdered men and the man who had murdered them, and Sylvia was talking as if she had been opening a bazaar. Sylvia *would*.

Gay shivered, and was glad when Algy came and sat on the arm of the big chair and put a hand on her shoulder. It had been perfectly horrible, but at least Algy was cleared, and Sylvia was apparently going to get off scot free. She had given her evidence with a good deal of inconsequent charm. She had looked ethereally lovely in her black. Her voice had faltered in all the right places, and she had wept when she described the scene in the yew walk. The Coroner had asked her a great many questions, but neither he nor anyone else had so much as mentioned the Home Secretary's lost memorandum. As far as this inquest went, it had never been stolen, and Lady Colesborough could not be supposed to have known of its existence.

She had been blackmailed by Mr Zero on account of a card debt which she did not want to confess to her husband. Sylvia had been very convincing about this. She told the Coroner just how difficult she found it to remember what were trumps. A tear fell when she admitted that Francis had forbidden her to play. And she had played. And she had lost. Five hundred pounds. And she had been so dreadfully afraid that Mr Zero would tell Francis. So she had taken a packet of letters out of her husband's safe. And so forth and so on. Not a word about the visit to Wellings and the Home Secretary's despatch-case. The Coroner led her gently but firmly through the pathetic tale. Sylvia left the court with the admiration and sympathy of everyone present. Tomorrow the Press would feature her as the lovely Lady Colesborough. Really it wasn't surprising that she should heave that gentle sigh and say how marvellously it had all gone off.

"Monty's been marvellous too," said Algy, for Gay's ear.

Gay stuck her chin in the air.

"I don't see what he's got to be marvellous about."

"Well, it hasn't been all jam for him. He offered to resign, you know, but they wouldn't let him. By the way, it puzzled me how Brewster could have known that Monty had got that memorandum and was taking it down to Wellings. You see, we were in the library,

Carstairs, Brewster, and myself, and Monty was up in his room. Carstairs went out into the hall, took the envelope from the messenger, and gave it to me to take up to Monty. That's what started them suspecting me. I had the handling of it. I knew what it was. I could have substituted the blank envelope which was found in the despatch-case at Wellings, or I could have rung up someone who was going to Wellings and told them to go ahead, the paper would be there. Now Brewster was doing statistics at the far end of the library. He never had a smell of the paper, and as far as my knowledge went he couldn't have known that it had arrived, or that Monty had taken it with him."

Gay shivered. She didn't want to talk about Mr Brewster — who was Mr Zero — who was dead. She said rather faintly, "How did he know?"

"Carstairs told him. Beautifully simple — isn't it? Carstairs approved of Brewster. He didn't approve of me, chiefly because I'm Monty's cousin and his Roman soul abhors the thought of family interest. Therefore he was quite sure that if anyone was playing the fool it must be me. Very hot on the trail was Carstairs, and he never said a word about having told Brewster that the memorandum had come and that Monty was taking it to Wellings until Brewster had blown his brains out and he couldn't go on approving of him any more. Mind you, he really did think I'd taken the damned thing. He's vindictive, but he's honest. And now I step into Brewster's shoes, and he'll never cease regretting him."

Sylvia shut the vanity case with which she had been busy. She had taken off her hat and her hair shone like pale gold. There were faint shadows under her lovely eyes. Her delicate pallor was unstained by rouge, but she had touched her lips with coral. She said,

"I suppose you really are engaged?"

A little flame burned in Gay's cheeks.

"I've been telling you so about twenty times a day ever since it happened."

"I know, darling, but people do say these things — don't they?"

Algy looked across at her with a sparkle in his eye.

"We have Monty's blessing, I have written to all my relations, we have cabled the glad news to Gay's parents, Aunt Agatha is in process of being de-iced, and there will be an announcement in the *Times* tomorrow. If there is anything else you can suggest —"

Sylvia smiled a little vaguely. Algy sometimes made her feel as if he was laughing at her, and she found that rather confusing, because there was nothing to laugh at. She began to think about what she would wear at the wedding. Not black — but they mustn't get married too soon. She said in a plaintive voice,

"How long will it be before I can come to your wedding? I mean, I wouldn't like to do anything that wasn't *right*. I mean, poor Francis — well, you know what I mean."

Also available in ISIS Large Print:

Murder Imperfect

Lesley Cookman

Pantomime director Libby Sarjeant has her hands full combining direction and detection when she's asked to look into threatening letters sent to Harry's gay friend Cy. At first she believes it to be a simple case of prejudice, but soon Libby uncovers links to particularly nasty crimes in the past, revelations that have catastrophic effects.

ISBN 978-0-7531-8862-0 (hb)
ISBN 978-0-7531-8863-7 (pb)

Ladies' Bane

Patricia Wentworth

Ladies' Bane — it was a curious name for a house. But visiting it for the first time Ione found it a curious house. Curious, and rather frightening. They said in the village that anyone who was its mistress would lose the thing she cared for most. And its present mistress was Allegra — Ione's sister.

They had not met for two years. Appointments had been made but not kept. Visits had been postponed time and time again. There had been excuse after excuse. And then suddenly Ione found herself not only invited but positively urged to come. To begin with she had been puzzled. But soon she was not only worried, but badly, deeply scared . . . Thank heavens Miss Silver was in town.

ISBN 978-0-7531-8704-3 (hb)
ISBN 978-0-7531-8705-0 (pb)